THIS ENDLESS ROAD

MICHAEL OVERA

Published by Unsolicited Press
www.unsolicitedpress.com
info@unsolicitedpress.com

Attention schools and businesses: for discounted copies
on large orders, please contact the publisher directly.

ISBN: 978-1-947021-20-4

For those that realize you need no ticket for a vacation into the stranger parts of your own mind (granted, a drink cart would be appreciated).

Contents

THIS
ENDLESS
ROAD

<u>This Endless Road</u>

The overnight Greyhound from San Antonio is a piss smelling thing crowded with the boredom of the thousands who have worn the seats threadbare over the years. Rita has been unable to sleep, and by the time the bus stops in a nowhere town somewhere in New Mexico, she drags herself from a precarious half-sleep. She's starving and the only thing open at six in the morning is a diner a half block from the bus depot, one of those places obligated to spring up along the highway at nearly perfect intervals, all vinyl booths and syrup stained tables that might as well have been pre-manufactured. She sits at the long counter next to the only other patron, a middle-aged trucker type with a face carved and eroded by wind, time, and sun. It's a face eroded by the open road, she thinks, and is surprised when she strikes up a conversation. Perhaps it's the particular nature of the stress and exhaustion that prompts her to spool out white lie after white lie. She tells him she is headed to Seattle to see a brother that doesn't exist in a place she's never been. It's simply a place unfathomably different from the arid, nearly treeless landscape of the Southwest. And so, she's just as surprised when he offers her a ride as far north as Oregon.

"You a serial killer?"

"Might ask the same of you," he smiles.

"Stranger danger, you know."

"Up to you," he says, sipping his coffee.
"Billy."

"Rita."

"Now we're not strangers."

"Doesn't really answer that whole serial killer question."

His eyes –pale blue – have a milkiness offset by his deep tan and crow's feet. Now, not a half-hour after meeting this stranger, she is sitting in the passenger seat of his battered Econoline-van, soaking in the smell of diesel and dust and cigarettes. The smell is so thick that when he first goes to light a cigarette she is certain that the whole van is going to go up in flames. Perhaps mistaking her expression for something else he rolls down the window, and the breeze stirs his salt-and pepper hair as he squints at the road.

There is no map beside him and he seems to chart a course by familiar or former landmarks; a string of forgotten towns that must form a constellation from Flagstaff to Albuquerque. Rita crumples her sweatshirt into a ball and tucks it between her shoulder and the window. The van is far too loud for music, let alone conversation, and the white noise of road hum coaxes her to sleep.

When she wakes again, Albuquerque has receded behind them by some unknown quantity of miles and minutes. It's a change in the road that wakes her—the smoothness of the highway giving way to rutted asphalt. She glances across at Billy, trying to trace her thoughts back to the diner – trying to shake the disorientation of waking in a moving vehicle next to someone she barely remembers meeting. A quarter mile down the road debris begins to appear, mixed in among the hardscrabble sage and spindly cacti. Unidentifiable rusting things caught naked beneath a high, accusatory sun. A low-slung Rambler comes into view, its white paint molting in thick flakes. Billy parks in front of the detached garage and, before he even ratchets up the parking break, a pair of black labs are circling the van – their coats chalky with dust. Threads of ropey drool dangle from their muzzles.

Rita steps down from the van, turning her head towards the sound of a screen door banging open. A tall, beer-paunched man emerges from the house, his long beard brushing his collar bone, his bald head shining.

"Don't worry," Billy says while patting the dogs, "he's friendly. And I don't just mean the dogs. Daltry, this is Rita. Rita, Daltry."

Rita smiles cautiously as the two men shake hands, the dogs sniffing at her feet until Daltry shoos them away, rattling a large wad of keys until he finds the one he's looking for and plugs it into a padlock on the front of the garage. The doors open outwards like old barn doors, and the flattened dirt has curved gouges where rocks have been dragged along their trajectory. At the front of the garage is a large motorcycle that, given the beastly size and chrome and dark leather, Rita assumes is a Harley. Beyond that there are makeshift tables – little more than sagging plywood propped up on old saw horses. Each table is crowded with odds and ends that, to her, would be considered junk.

As the lights overhead stutter to life she can decipher dozens of old appliances, mechanical and electrical things, most of which probably don't work anymore. The lines of the older machines betray a long-gone period: substantial curving metal like the true lines of vintage cars. The look of appliances that were intended to perch on countertops in the most modern homes are juxtaposed against the newer more angular plastic models. To Rita, it's less appliance graveyard than archeological curiosity.

Billy pulls a pair of glasses from his breast pocket and perches them on his nose. The glasses lend him a grandfatherly look as he makes a slow circuit around the table. Along the

far wall a workbench is crowded with parts and
tools and other unidentifiable detritus of
someone who has horded machines and tools for
years. Nothing here matches, and the only order
seems to be disorder.

"Looks a mess, don't it?" Billy asks without
looking at Rita. "Guarantee Daltry here can find
anything he wants in this place. Could probably
even tell you the story of most everything in
here."

"Here," Daltry says, pulling back a canvas
tarp, "this is what I was telling you about."

As the tarp is pulled back it reveals an old
pinball machine its sides painted in bright
yellows and reds. Stylized demons leer from the
sides of the machine, its glass backboard
designed to match. No doubt generations of kids
have leaned over the machine frantically
tapping the little round buttons, for a moment
drawn into a world composed only of the
duration of a quarter and the clack of the
flippers. She can't remember how long it's been
since she'd seen one like this.

"Stuck relays?"
"It's what made me think you might be
interested. Pretty sure the problem is the
electrics. I could fix it up, but no way is it going
to sell around here. Better to ship it off to one of
those specialty shops."

"Seems to be in good shape otherwise."

Rita jiggles the switch on an old blender, runs her hand along the cord to its frayed end. Angling the gooseneck of a lamp, she tries to imagine who the machine belonged to: a student bent over hours of homework, or a tired father endlessly paying bills. Maybe it illuminated the daily progression of domestic paperwork that accumulated in sheaves or scattered like old leaves. In the corner, by the pinball machine, Billy and Daltry are haggling over the price in a way that seems comfortable and familiar; she can tell this is sport. A simple game. When they have settled on a price, they set to work wordlessly to dismantle the thing and carry the pieces out to the van. While they work, Rita crouches by the garage doors, speaking to the dogs in secret whispers; it's the first time she's been able to breathe since she left.

The back of the van is already crowded with machines that Billy must have picked up in Albuquerque or Lubbock. An antique Coca-Cola machine lays flat on its back, held in place by its own tremendous weight. Power tools are heaped into battered cardboard boxes, their cords coiled like sleeping snakes. The men sweat and curse as they shimmy and angle the pieces into place and tie them down with broad nylon straps. All these things in the back of the van are things she hasn't noticed until now.

Billy slams the door closed and the two men light cigarettes standing silently beneath the high, bright sun. Billy slips his glasses into his pocket. His naked eyes crinkle as he squints into the late morning. After a few minutes, the men crush out their cigarettes and shake hands in a truncated goodbye, syllables slipping from their lips like left over smoke. And then Billy is guiding the van back onto the northbound highway.

"This is your job?"

"It's a living. I don't know if it counts as a real regular job type job."

If he had mentioned something about travelling across the states, scavenging things he could fix, it had been in her earlier state of exhaustion. Now that same exhaustion settles into her temples, fuzzing her vision. There are scraps and fragments that come back to her now: retired for a several years, a military pension collected after serving twenty-five years in the Navy, something about the road reminding him of the ocean. For some unknown reason, either out of survival instinct or courtesy, she struggles against exhaustion. She has to lean towards him and shout to be heard.

"You have a wife and kids?"

"Not that sort of guy."

"Guess not."

"You?"

"Ex-husband back in Austin. No kids."

He nods distractedly, but whether it's because she has been convincing or because he doesn't care, she couldn't tell. The conversation slides into silence as they pass and repass the same cars for miles at a time. The road unwinds in front of them like a great, black spool of ribbon that sometimes rolls straight through the desert and at other times bends awkwardly over the hills; folding back on itself in switchbacks that cause the engine to deepen its pitch until Billy finally downshifts. She is in and out of sleep. Sometime that first full day, after waking up again, she reaches over to where his pack of Marlboros shiver on the dashboard and draws one from the pack. Billy only nods and punches in the plastic button of the cigarette lighter with his knuckle. It's the first cigarette she's had in over five years, and the raw, burnt-marshmallow taste of the thing coats her mouth and throat. She closes her eyes and lets the dappled red dots of sun play against the curtain of her eyelids.

The sun begins to paint the western sky tangerine as they cross into Utah. By Cedar City the sky has been painted over again with a deep blue that edges towards black. They take an off-ramp and Rita roles down the window, the cooling breeze goose-pimpling her skin. Her

face is dry and warm and her arms are newly
sunburned pink.

They stop briefly in a supermarket, easing
into a parking space in an almost empty lot.
Captured heat radiates up off of the asphalt.
There's an almost salty smell in the air. Then it
is the hush of the automatic doors opening and
the crispness of air conditioning. The cracked
linoleum of the floors, lackluster produce, and a
harsh bright light that makes everything look
startling real. Here Rita buys a few packs of
cigarettes and the essentials that she's somehow
forgotten: toothbrush, soap, deodorant. These
things look stark and mundane as she stands
behind Billy, noticing the way the scraggly gray
hairs at the base of his neck stand out against
his tanned skin crisscrossed with a web of
creases. The tan and the creases the result of
hours leaning over the steering wheel or peering
intently into one machine or another.

It's late, and there is something else now
that she hasn't thought about, that they must
sleep somewhere. Cedar City seems like a ghost
town as they follow the highway east. They spot
the flashing neon of a "vacancy" sign." A motel
clings to the isolation of the highway, the
streetlights highlighting the seemingly
inevitable and lackluster stucco outside.

"Back in a minute," he says.

"I'll come in with you."

"I'll see to it."

Perhaps, she thinks, this is some semblance of self-preservation. She could easily be mistaken for a prostitute. A derelict or a runaway. There must be some specific word for this, the women that hitch rides from one town to another paying their way with sex. She remembers the bumper sticker now, the one that her brother had plastered to the back of his truck: "Gas, Grass, or Ass, no one rides for free." Is it really that? Would someone really think of her as some sort of freeway whore?

Inside the motel room, a chugging AC churns decades of stale cigarette smoke; a smell that lords over the narrow beds and the pink and green flecked carpet. The room itself is shabby in the same way that everything in the town seems shabby. Shabby in a way that betrays countless years of feet treading grooves in the carpet. Shabby from the countless cigarettes smoked and absorbed into the walls and blankets until no amount of laundry detergent or bleach will ever make the sheets truly clean again. Though the beds are well made and sheathed in carefully smoothed floral comforters, the whole room is nearly frigid. Billy sits at the edge of the bed closest to the door and retrieves a pint of whiskey from his duffle and pours a hefty slug into one of the plastic cups that have been left beside the sink. As he holds out the bottle to her she shakes her head.

"Think I'm going to shower first."

"Don't take all the hot water," he says while unlacing his work boots and dropping them unceremoniously to the floor.

Rita closes and locks the bathroom door, although both door and lock are flimsy things. She can hear the TV come on in the other room, the sound merging with the air conditioner and the ceiling fan and the rush of the shower. She stands for a moment watching the water pool around the drain before stripping out of her sweat-damp tank top and clammy jeans. Her body, so familiar, feels like a borrowed dress – a hand-me-down from a forgotten self –as she steps into the shower, letting the water soak into her skin, washing away road dust and regret. She watches the water as it stutters over her stretch marks. Slowly, almost reluctantly, she pushes the thin bar of hotel soap over her skin, forcing it into a lather. The sudden cold of the water drags her from her daze and she finds herself sitting on the bottom of the tub. Reaching up, she turns off the water, lifts herself up, and pulls a frayed white towel from the metal shelf above the toilet. She presses the towel to her face, ruffles her hair, squeegees the steam from the mirror and stands there staring at her reflection for a long moment. Her hair, free from its pony tail, hangs in limp tendrils around her face as she dresses in yesterday's clothes.

Back in the room, the TV casts a blue glow on the far wall and she can hear Billy snoring softly. She pauses there in the doorway of the bathroom and weighs the decision to turn off the TV, waffling. It's better, she finally decides, to leave it on.

In the semi-darkness, she listens to the stranger's cartoon snore and tries to make sense of this wanderer, a man relegated to the road, who has decided to pick up a woman half his age in a diner without any expectation of anything more. There is nothing in him to indicate that he might be dangerous – and maybe she trusted him only on a semi-suicidal impulse. Ever since she left San Antonio, now well over twenty-four hours before, she promised herself that she wouldn't play things safe or logical. There is no point in that now. Maybe it's a turn towards the ascetic, she tells herself. The amphetamine edge of guilt is blunted by shear exhaustion as her wet hair soaks into the pillow.

She wakes without realizing that she has been asleep. As she eases into consciousness she looks around the room, half expecting the soft blue walls of her bedroom back in San Antonio. She expects Travis to be lying beside her. Even before she is fully awake, as she lingers in the

no-man's land that stretches between sleep and
wakefulness, she realizes that she isn't at home.
The bed is slightly too cool and the comforter is
slightly too scratchy. There is the stale scent of
cheap soap, industrial cleaner, and cigarettes.
And then she is acutely aware of Billy leaning
against the frame of the open door smoking a
cigarette, his back towards her. Just past him,
outside, she can see the pale morning light
straining over the torn paper hills of the horizon
as the sun chases away the last of the night. A
dull drone of nearby traffic. She eases out of
bed, an unintentional groan escaping her lips,
and Billy glances over his shoulder.

"Morning."

"It looks that way," she says.

Billy snorts and crushes out his cigarette in
the oversized glass ashtray in the middle of the
table. He is dressed in a plaid shirt that, at first,
she thinks is the same one from yesterday.
There is some subtle difference in color and
pattern, though. Rita brushes her hair quickly,
pulling at the snarls and snags with staticky
snaps before sweeping it back into a ponytail
that she knows will be loose and sloppy before
the end of the hour. She shoves her things down
into her backpack, quickly brushes her teeth
and rolls on deodorant. Billy is patient, standing
outside the room sipping coffee from a
Styrofoam cup. She emerges, shoulders her bag,

and hands her room key to Billy. She stands beside the van smoking one of his cigarettes as he walks to the front office to return their keys. The van is cold from the desert night and she shivers down into her sweatshirt, huddling into herself as she waits. The desert always seems too bright in the morning – as if there has been no transition between night and day. She squints at the other cars, mute and dust coated, like lonely husks.

They make a quick stop at a filling station a stone's throw from Veterans Memorial Highway. The name had stuck with her when she'd first seen it beneath the blue freeway signs. The red crown above the white fifteen. As he fills the tank she slips inside the tiny convenience store. She thinks about how easy it would be for him to climb into the van and drive away, stranding her in an unfamiliar place. No one knows her here. She has little more than the modest stack of bills in her wallet, nestled in a slowly crumpling white envelope. Or she could leave him. She could wander off, or lock herself in the bathroom and out wait him. A part of her wonders if she has a secret desire to be left here. How easy it would be to disappear out the back door of the convenience store and go meandering down the back alleys of this anonymous town. There is a certain lightness in the disconnection; she is unmoored from any responsibility of past

or future. But she returns to the van and sets
one coffee in the oversized cup holders and curls
her fingers around her own cup, soaking in
every bit of warmth that seeps through the
cardboard.

The only real company they have for the
next hour is the number of semis that they leap-
frog up and down the highway; semis that
displace walls of air that rock the van from side
to side. They trace 15 North and she imagines
that she can tell the locals by the way that they
speed past in casually dented cars. She finishes
a bag of chips from the gas station, crumples the
empty bag, and tosses it onto the floorboards
where it mingles with the other debris that has
accumulated: empty packs of cigarettes and
soda cans, candy wrappers and convenience
store bags. Squat, brown signs with stark white
lettering for Yuba State Park start to appear by
the side of the road.

"Ever been?"

"Yuba?"

"Maybe we could stop."

She tries to convince herself now that this is
more a trip than an escape. There is something
about stopping here at the roadside state park
that validates her leaving. At least she can say
that she has seen something she never would
have seen in San Antonio. Another sign comes

into view and Billy begin to slow, downshifting as he eases along the off ramp and into the park itself.

A reservoir expands before them like an uneven mirror dotted with sailboats and inner tubes. Clusters of tents are perched on the pale, flat dunes and Billy coasts to a stop in the small parking lot. The white noise evaporates and now they are stuck with the sudden awkwardness of not having anything to say to each other. The engine ticks silently as Billy hangs his arm out the window, a curlicue of smoke making its way past the side mirror.

"People drive past places like this," she says.

In response is only a nearly imperceptible nod. The soft breeze off the reservoir dances her own cigarette smoke out the window in little waltzing movements and she opens the door and climbs down onto the asphalt. Heat radiates up off the blacktop in shimmering waves.

"Looks like there might be a better view over here," she says, pointing to where the dunes rise and merge into the high pine trees.

"Go ahead," Billy says, "I'mma get twenty winks."

Rita follows a narrow dirt trail that emerges in a small shady area near a tent set on the high ground beneath the trees. Farther down, along the shore, a man fusses with a hibachi while a woman in a lawn chair intermittently watches two young boys as they run and squeal and splash in the shallow water at the edge of the reservoir. The pale, round bellies of the boys protrude over their brightly colored, matching swim trunks. She can't help but notice that the boys are only a few years younger than Caleb as she steps down to the shore not far from where they are playing.

Stepping out of her shoes, she lets the timid waves lap around her toes and ankles. She imagines wading out there, farther and farther into the cool water, allowing it to envelope her an inch at a time. The level would rise up her calves and thighs until, eventually, she would be weightless and the warm surface layer of water would give way to the deeper, cooler water just beneath. She could dive down deeper and deeper until her lungs burned and her muscles cramped. There in the thick darkness she would roll onto her back, allowing the water to hem her in, and look through the murky water towards the shimmering surface. Exhaled air would bubble from her throat, passing through her lips like unarticulated secrets and she would begin to sink until she was stored up behind the dam with the silt and silence; insulated by thousands upon thousands of gallons of water and upstream refuse.

Behind her on the shore the woman begins shouting to the boys, and the sharpness of her voice pulls Rita back to the present. She glances up and makes fleeting and accidental eye contact from the woman, causing them both to look away abruptly. Back at the van, Billy is reclining in the driver's seat, his head tilted back. As she nears the parking lot she thinks of Travis back at home, no doubt wondering where she's gone. She imagines him sitting at the kitchen table, having finally found the note that she left for him in the picture frame beside the bed. She tries to chase these ideas away as she opens the passenger side door and climbs back up into the cab. Billy opens his eyes and grips the steering wheel to pull himself forward.

"Good walk?"

Rita nods abstractly as she brushes the sand from the bottoms of her feet and shakes out her shoes before putting them back on. Billy turns the key and the van is alive again and they are slowly pulling back out of the spot. She knows that there, beyond the dunes, the two young boys are still splashing at the edge of the water. The man is still fussing with the hibachi and the woman is still looking up intermittently to check on the boys. Drifting in the middle of the lake, a man reclines in the bow of an old rowboat, the invisible line from his fishing rod creating concentric circles where it enters the water.

They cross and re-cross the Snake River, following 86 as it cuts west, passing through towns with names like Rupert, Heyburn, Mountain Home. The sky darkens and the clouds crumple into different shades of black and gray as the air becomes electric. After a few miles, Rita rolls up her window and wraps the sweatshirt around her shoulders. She can't help but think of the thunderstorms back in Texas. She thinks of the way that the small, fine hairs on her arms would begin to prickle in the hour or two before a thunderhead rolled across town. She thinks of the time that she had walked out onto the front porch with Caleb in her arms. He had been a little more than a year-old then, but he was quiet and calm in her arms as they stood there watching the distant flashes and counting together in anticipation of the accompanying thunder. Even the slowest build and rumble and snap didn't startle Caleb as he looked up at her and twisted his head to the side to stare at the distant landscape. The lights had flashed off their faces and ephemeral shadows pirouetted on the flat landscape. Travis had thought that she was crazy for that, keeping a young child out in a thunderstorm. For nearly an hour Rita stood out there with Caleb, and Travis stood behind them, just inside the screen door shifting nervously from foot to foot until they finally came inside.

Now it is that same familiar electricity that prickles her skin and lets her know that the storm will start soon – a certain type of barometric pressure on her skin and she can't help but smile. Soon enough, the light crackles on the distant landscape in strobing, bright flashes, too far away for the thunder to reach them. After another mile, the rain seems to assault the van from all sides.

"Some storm," Billy says.

"How much more do we have?"

"Another hour or so."

The place, Caldwell, isn't far off the freeway, and Billy pulls down a side street past boxy 1950s houses painted in light blues and pale greens. They pass houses painted in off whites and barely grays, until finally he parks along the curb in front of a pale blue rambler with a scuffed front door. The rain has slackened by now, but the asphalt is a black mirror. A creosote smell lingers– the concrete has been dry for months, she can tell. The woman that answers the door is, as best as Rita can tell, about Billy's age and the two of them embrace in a casual way that makes Rita realize that she has never shared any form of physical contact with the man – not so much as a hand shake.

Billy introduces the woman as Nancy, an old friend, as the woman ushers them inside and takes their bags and sets them in a small office off the hallway before leading them into the kitchen where a man in a wheelchair stirs a steaming pot. The men shake hands affably and Billy introduces him as his old Navy buddy, Paul. Rita can't help but wonder if it is the Navy that landed Paul in his wheelchair, but she knows that it is something that she can't ask. She knows this just as much as she knows that it is unlikely that she'll learn the cause for the wheelchair anytime in the next twelve hours or so that they are in Caldwell. It's a place she may never see again, and people she may never meet again. Nancy hands her a can of cold beer and then they are all lighting cigarettes and talking as Paul putters about in the kitchen refusing any offer for help. The house itself is cramped; the space between furniture has been engineered to be just wide enough for Paul's chair to pass through, but otherwise the whole place is vaguely claustrophobic. Nancy wants to know how Rita ended up riding with Billy and Billy relates the story.

"Thought maybe you two were lovers," says Nancy.

"Jesus, Nan." Paul says.

"An honest question."

"It's all right," Rita smiles.

"You said you were from Texas?"

"Bad divorce."

"Best thing for it is to get away," Nancy says. "So, no kids?"
Rita shakes her head and the conversation moves through dinner and the history that Paul and Billy and Nancy shares extends far beyond Rita's reality. From what she can piece together, the two men met in the Navy. The stories are from different ports and other sailors and it's difficult to track the fragmented memories, a jumble of forgotten names and barely remembered anecdotes. There are stories that pre-date Nancy and she shakes her head as they begin, knowing the trajectory of the stories from the first word like an overplayed song and will even fill in details that the men forget to include. Rita smiles and jiggles her foot under the table as she smokes and listens and smokes and listens. Each story that unfolds reveals a foreign truth, like a window she has glanced through by accident. It's a voyeuristic thing, and she can't help but wonder if this is simply the natural unfolding of life. Rita thinks of how nice it would be to exist only as a footnote in someone else's life —and wants desperately now to negate the world that she is a part of. If she is lucky, one day she will be only a half-remembered anecdote told over cheap beer and cheaper cigarettes.

By midnight beer cans have crowded out their elbowroom on the table and the four of them go on tapping cigarette ash into empty cans and talking and laughing too loudly until Nancy hazards a glance at the clock on the stove. It's late she says and they all agree, reluctant to end their evening, although the air in the kitchen is thick with exhaled blue smoke and eyelids are beginning to droop. It's probably time for them to all turn in, especially if Billy and Rita want to get an early start, although the thought of an early start is odd to Rita, who has no specific destination or deadline. Rita follows Nancy into the small office where the two of them work together to unfold the hide-a-bed and spread the sheets over the creased mattress. They work in quiet unison transforming what must be Paul's office into a guest room. There is a broad desk near the window that looks out on the backyard, and the desk is populated with knives and chisels and half-carved figurines and a small plastic pallet of paint.

"Can I get you anything else?"

Rita shakes her head as Nancy eases the door nearly closed, leaving only a gap that reveals a sliver of hallway. Rita's mother used to leave the same type of gap in her bedroom door when she was a girl; it's the same type of gap that she would leave after putting Caleb to bed.

In her underwear and a mostly clean T-shirt, she crawls beneath the cool covers and wishes that she could stay – as if, even as an adult, she could be adopted by these near strangers. The patchwork quilt stretches and ripples over her legs as she thinks of Caleb far away, however many miles distant, in his room hating her, thinking of her, struggling to understand.

She can hear Nancy out in the front room making up a bed for Billy on the couch. There is the rustle and snap of blankets unfurling and Rita can hear the muffled murmurs of their voices, and, somewhere else, she hears what must be Paul maneuvering his chair towards a bed. She hears or imagines the spring squeak of a well-worn bed, and hears a door closed and hushed voices that are only mouse-like mutterings in the walls. Rita turns towards the window and can tell that the storm has moved off, farther to the west, leaving behind only a light rain that scatters timidly across the windows.

A long line of amber peeps through the window and bends over the foot of the bed, signaling that the rain has stopped. What woke her is not the light, but the sound of hushed voices in the kitchen. Or, maybe it is the smell of coffee and toast and eggs. She dresses and pulls the blankets from the hide-a-bed and folds them into uneven squares and stacks them on the edge of the mattress. As she pauses there by the door, trying to build up her nerve, she can hear the crinkle of a newspaper and for a moment is shocked that people still have newspapers delivered. When she steps into the hallway, she can see the three of them sitting there over squares of newspaper folded into discrete sections. She watches, like a voyeur, the way Nancy lays her hand on Paul's shoulder as she pours his coffee. It reminds her of a past less than a week old – but there is already a heavy callous forming between past and present self.

It's after eight by the time they are carrying their bags out to the van. In the wake of the storm the morning is a luminous golden thing with high clear skies. Paul and Nancy watch from the porch as Billy fires up the van and the two of them wave one more time before the van edges away from the curb. Suddenly self-conscious, Rita glances at Billy trying to find a particular beat in the steady silence; a moment to say something, if only she could think of something to say. Beat after beat passes. Each time she is about ready to speak, she loses her resolve. For a moment, she thinks that she will tell him everything. She will tell him about her husband and her son. But she will not be able to answer the one real question.

"You've known them a long time," she says finally.

"Years."

She wants to believe that beneath his truncated statement there is a current of memory that drags him back all the way to the time before Paul's accident, and now it sounds less real and more like the name of painting: Paul Before Chair. In the painting the two men stand side-by-side, grinning in their starched white Navy uniforms with their little round caps. But there are private things that she will never learn about them, and she knows that there is an entire cache of memories that belong to a person and that those memories, like the person themselves, can never be fully excavated, no matter how relentless the questioning. There is a part of each person, she thinks, that must remain an unknowable and unreachable Shangri-La. Some inaccessible place where the true-truth hides.

But now they are nearing the freeway and the silence will soon be overridden by road noise and so she takes the last few minutes to ask where they are heading. Somewhere north, Billy says, close to Seattle.

"Figure I might as well take you all the way."

Rita grabs the pack of cigarettes from the dash and punches in the lighter and stares at it until the little button pops out. She wants to ask

him why Seattle, and then she remembers that
Seattle is where she told him she's headed to.
She wants to tell him that he needn't bother.
There is nothing in Seattle for her. She has
never been. Before she can tell him, she realizes
that she is beginning to rely on him, and it
scares her. It seems too much like the same
direction that she has come from. Maybe there
is some way in which she has unwittingly tied
herself to this stranger, becoming connected
when she hasn't intended to. It's how she ended
up with Travis in the first place, coasting
through acquaintanceship to friendship and
relationship. A relationship that was a steady
gravitational pull rather than love-at-first-site-
Hollywood-Romance. And then that same
gravitational pull locked her into Travis's orbit
and she was stuck forever encircling him. For a
moment, she thinks that she will call Travis
from the next gas station that they come to.
She'll begin to apologize but he will insist, in his
usual way, that he has already forgiven her.

She will stand in a dry, sand-swept parking
lot sweating under late afternoon sun, heat
shivering the asphalt, cars ticking over the
expansion joints in the freeway. Travis will
careen into the parking lot in his sensible sedan
and park in front of her, the car still running,
the door hanging open as he wraps his arms
around her. She sees it now from a bird's eye

view, like a Hollywood delusion. He'll hold her and tell her that he forgave her before she even hung up the phone. He forgave her as soon as he heard her voice. Travis will have left Caleb at home. He would be unable to bear it. Once at home, Caleb will be harder to appease. But the only thing that matters now is that she is back and that they are together and that nothing can pull them apart and all this craziness can be put firmly behind them. In a few years, maybe, they'll be laughing about the whole thing. A diminishing memory.

But that won't happen, she tells herself. There is a filament stretching from her to Travis and Caleb that is stretched so taut that it is on the verge of snapping. The tension pulls against her heart, and she knows that as soon as it breaks she will be forever liberated. She simply has to be patient and wait for the days and miles to insulate her from her past. This is the hardest part, she tells herself as she crushes out one cigarette and lights another.

"You all right?" Billy asks.

"Sure."

"Just checking. You seem… I'm not sure what the word is."

"Pensive?"

"Pensive. Thinking about something. Texas maybe."

"You know how it is," she says.

It's an empty phrase half shouted in the inside of a strange van in a place she never thought she'd be, and she realizes that he doesn't know and couldn't know, not truly, not ever. Thankfully, Billy remains true to form, running at almost absolute Radio Silence. Outside the window, the landscape begins to change slowly, but definitely. There are more hills now, and the ranches and farms are dotted with pastured horses and cows.

The van passes a rumbling semi and they follow the winding highway as it runs, at least for the time being, parallel to old railroad tracks. The day on the road has a familiar rhythm by now, like the grooves worn in the highway – abrade by hundreds of thousands of cars. Except for the changing license plates and scenery, they would be caught in the doldrums of nowhere America – the road stretching backwards and forwards inexorably. They stop only for gas and the routine is identical even if the names of the stations change. Billy stands at the pump arching his back, trying to pop the lowest vertebrate. Or he stretches over the hood of the van to scrape bugs from the windshield. Or he taps the overfull ashtray into an overfull garbage can. Inside the convenience store, Rita scores the shelves for candy and beef jerky and chips. Buys the ubiquitous beer and cigarettes.

The desert landscape of Eastern Washington is somehow familiar: the same pickups and cowboy hats and gun racks. It had never occurred to her that there might be a rural part of Washington; in her mind the entire state was one sprawling metropolitan. An endless Seattle. The reality of it is that the bulk of the state is broad and empty as the deserted lacunae of Texas. For miles at a time, blacktop roads crisscross the crumpled landscape, adorned with little roadside attractions that you see in horror movies or out of tabloids, advertising two headed lizards and mummified Indian chiefs.

A column of military trucks passes them, rumbling in mismatched tans and dark greens. The soldiers behind the high flat windows are anonymous in their helmets and uniforms. There's no doubt in her mind that some of them are veterans, although to Rita they look impossibly young, like kids playing pretend. A few miles later, Billy pulls off of the highway and into the parking lot of yet another cheap motel. It's the first motel that hasn't been made almost entirely out of stucco and surrounded by depressed cacti. The single queen bed doesn't bother her either, even as Billy apologizes and insists – as if to reassure himself – that he will sleep on the floor. Rita considers, momentarily, turning on the TV but decides against it, hoping that the comfortable silence of the van will settle into the room, but even after hours of driving together in close proximity there is a pronounced awkwardness. They are no longer distracted by the unscrolling of the asphalt. There is no road hum to screen potential conversation. There is no anticipation of a destination other than sleep.

Billy drains his glass, downing the last bit of whiskey that he has poured evenly into two glasses. Amber droplets ripple around the edge as Billy squints and rubs his eyelids with grease cracked thumb and forefinger. He tilts the bottle and turns it slowly so that the unclaimable residue of alcohol chases itself around the inside of the bottle, and then, unceremoniously, he pitches it into the plastic waste basket with the thud of finality. She can tell that the end-of-day sobriety makes him acutely aware of his aching back and dry eyes.

"Saw a gas station a mile or so back up the road," he says.

"You want company?

Billy shakes his head and grabs his keys from the nightstand. She can hear his heavy boots on the metal stairs as he thumps down to the parking lot and then, after a moment, she can hear the engine of the van as it turns over, and headlights sway across the room as he backs out of the spot. It's the first time that she's been alone since Yuba two days ago.

Rita opens her bag and spills the contents onto the faded bedspread. All of her meager clothes are dirty, but she no longer cares. Even so, she tells herself that she will wash her clothes in the sink and hang them in the bathroom to dry while they sleep. In the morning, she will pack the still damp clothes into her bag and drape them one at a time over the back of her seat while they drive. There, the clothes marinate in cigarette smell and exhaust.

Her slim red wallet is zippered into a side pocket of her backpack. Wanting a reminder of herself, she fishes the wallet out and slides her ID from its plastic sleeve. What she wants is to see herself – not who she is now – she wants to see who she was before leaving. She reads the address on her license and tries to picture the house. There is the photograph that she had pulled from the bedside frame before she left, and she runs a finger along the torn edge. It's a picture taken over a year ago. Not long after leaving, she tore Travis from the picture and let the fragment of him flutter out the window of a westbound Greyhound. She'd been afraid that the picture of him would stare at her accusatorily. But now it is Caleb, who is gazing at something just off to one side of the camera, which sears her heart. She struggles to recreate

the moment in her head, but it is a moss-
covered stone, an idea that has blurred at the
edges until the hard, definite lines have
softened into uncertainty.

Rita puts all of these things back into her
bag and takes a towel from the bathroom and
scribbles a note for Billy on the hotel stationary
left with the Gideon Bible in the nightstand.
This way he won't wonder where she's gone off
to. When they first pulled up to the hotel she'd
seen the rippling light of a pool on the high
brick walls. Now she is there, a day's worth of
captured heat breathing between her toes, as
she slips out of her clothes and lays them over a
lounge chair with her towel. Stripped to her
underwear, she wades out into the cool water
until she is sweeping her arms in broad, even
strokes. Her feet kicking lightly as the bottom of
the pool slopes away from her: four, five, six
feet. At the deep end of the pool she exhales
until all that is left in her lungs is an aching
tightness. She bounces softly against the
textured bottom of the pool, her hair tendriling
around her like pale smoke and the chlorine
stinging her eyes. She wants the weight of the
water pressing down on her now – the
unforgiving insistence. Tomorrow, she will step
out of the van at the next gas station, and she
will disappear, leaving Billy waiting there for
fifteen or twenty minutes until he finally ducks

inside the convenience store to check for her. He will wait by the ladies' restroom until a stranger emerges and looks at him with suspicion. And then he will return to the empty van and know that she is gone and the pain he feels will be a fraction of what it might have otherwise been.

Temporary Home

The turn off to Sunny Groves Trailer Park lies just off Route 82 and is shy of town by three or four miles. At the crest of the hill the road seems to stretch interminably towards the horizon. As a kid, Selena had looked forward to the monthly treks out there to visit her uncle, Patrick, but at some point, she realized that the whole place was atavistic. A place captured in the ambered kitsch of the last half of the 20th century. Everything in the park is a fragment of one forgotten era or another. The short, paved driveway quickly dissolves into gravel and the gravel quickly dissolves into a patchiness that is more dirt than gravel. It was a thing that had seemed almost fairy-tale-ish when she was younger. Now she sees it for the tattered relic that it is, and it depresses her, mostly because she holds it up against the quaint suburb where she grew up in.

Endless summers of her youth are marinated in the nostalgia of dust clouds chasing car tires until everything was coated in a chalky film that seemed to insulate the park from the rest of the world. It felt like being marooned on a tropical island. She can still remember the delightful disgust of Patrick's neighbor, a piratical and ancient man who liked to pop the glass eye out of his socket and roll it around in his mouth. But he was gone now. He'd been gone long before she was old enough to drive to the park on her own.

And still, Patrick's 72 Winnebago Brave is lodged there, beached as it were, in a back corner near the sagging chain link fence of the park. It was a shipwrecked thing that hadn't moved in at least the decade since he'd first parked it there in slip 19. Moss clung to the vinyl siding of the trailer and the tires had the bellied sag of surrender. Still, Selena revisits those vague memories—memories full of high white sun and squinted eyes, and the blinding dimness and cool interior of the trailer.

The first time Selena visited Patrick somewhere other than the trailer was when she went to visit him in Memorial Hospital, where he was already frail and looking decades older than his actual fifty-something years. The cancer carved away pounds of his flesh as if it was penance for decades of booze and cigarettes. That day in the hospital, Selena had placed her hand on his still sun-darkened arm, the skin warm and smooth beneath her fingers. The back of his left hand was puckered with a mottled purple bruise where too white gauze held the IV in place. He hadn't had much to say then and, instead, offered an exhausted smile; for once at a loss for words.

Patrick had lingered for several months –
May through August – and Selena did her best
to visit him on weekends before shifts at the
Red Apple on Main and 6th. It wasn't long before
he had convinced her to smuggle in airline
bottles of whiskey, which she would pass to him
surreptitiously after the nurse had left the
room. Her mother had been appalled when
Selena had mentioned it.

"What's it going to do," Selena asked. "Kill
him?"
His face sagged with weakness, but Patrick
could still wrangle his crooked grin whenever
she stepped into his room. He would struggle up
into a sitting position and joke that he'd been
wondering when she was going to come fill his
"prescription." It was a brave face, she knew.
This was a gift for her. He seemed unaware of
the bank of machines perched beside him like
sentries; each dragging its own jagged line
across a dark screen, a beeping chorus of
charted heart rate and blood pressure, one more
machine pumping mechanical breaths into his
lungs. The whole thing was antiseptic and
sterile and was about as far from humanity as
she could imagine any situation being. She
wondered, as she sat beside him those days
when he drifted off to sleep, how anyone could
die in a place that lacked any semblance of
comfort. It made sense to her now why people

chose to die at home, in familiar surroundings, rather than the stark blankness of a hospital that was little more than Death's antechamber.

"All these machines," he said one afternoon, stirring up from what she thought had been a terminal sleep, "maybe after all this they're going to make me into Darth Vader."

"You always did have a bit of Dark Side in you," she said, smiling.

Unintentionally, she began to believe that he would survive as long as he was linked to the immortality of those machines. Of course, if asked, she would have denied it. So, it was all the more a shock when she came home from work one February afternoon and saw her mother sitting at the kitchen table with crumpled tissues flowering before her and another twisted in and around her fingers.

Selena was angry that her mother hadn't called her at work to let her know, but she realized that there was little that could be done. The death was expected, after all, and Selena might as well have finished work. There would be plenty of time to work, and plenty of time to grieve. The dead, her father said, had an unfortunate way of remaining that way. But the true surprise came when a slightly overweight lawyer in a rumpled suit showed up at the

house and told Selena that she had inherited
Patrick's Winnebago. The lawyer rattled a wad
of keys in his hand and gestured to the briefcase
in his other hand. There was a protracted
silence.

"Mind if I come in?" he asked.

Inside the house, the two of them sat at the
kitchen table while the lawyer explained the
particulars. Patrick had called him not long
after being admitted to the hospital and made
out his last will and testament. The lawyer
explained that her uncle had first proposed
leaving everything to his tomcat. The lawyer
talked him out of it, and the next name out of
his mouth had been hers. The lawyer was
convinced that he'd planned on leaving it to her
this whole time. Selena doubted that anyone in
the family knew that there was a will or
anything to be inherited. As it turned out, the
inheritance was relegated to the Winnebago and
its contents. Maybe the remainder of a tab at
the Roadhouse where Patrick had spent most of
his nights with his fellow barflies. Once they'd
signed the requisite paper work, the lawyer
clicked his pen and slipped it back into his
breast pocket.

"You, young lady, are now the proud owner
of a 1972 Winnebago Brave."

That night Selena retreated to her basement bedroom after dinner and inserted a Jim Morrison album into the CD player. She sat there in the hazy smell of incense, illuminated by the glow from the crisscrossing Christmas lights she had strung in her junior year of high school. High school, only a few years in the past, seemed to be a lifetime ago. Staring at the twinkling reds and blues and greens of small light bulbs, she realized she might have spent the rest of her life in the basement if not for the sudden arrival of the Winnebago. It was as if the inheritance had been an omen, Patrick channeling his own hopes for freedom and independence. A call to the sea, he might have said.

And so, as Morrison's baritone started up the same album for a third time, she had resolved to move into the trailer. Her parents would be ambivalent about her moving, but she was twenty-two and a grown woman with a steady job. Maybe to her parents she was still a child, and she knew that a trailer park was an okay place for an alcoholic uncle, but not the type of place where they wanted their only daughter living alone.

"Stay as long as you want," her mother said as she laid a hand on Selena's arm. 'It's not as though you have to move out tomorrow."

"She wants her freedom," her father said. "Who can blame her for not moving out before this?"

"Well," her mother said, "you're close enough that you can come home anytime. This is still your home. Always will be."

The Monday following the lawyer's visit, Selena and her mother drove out to Sunny Groves Trailer park with a back seat crammed full of boxes. Loosely packed knick-knacks and high school trophies rattled faintly. She wasn't certain how to pack. She'd lived in that house for as long as she could remember. Now those crisp new boxes were crowded with jumbled memories: elementary school and middle school and high school. Half of her clothes still on their hangers, folded over each other in the trunk. Neither of them could remember when they'd last been out to the park, but the way was familiar and automatic, and they didn't have to talk about the specifics as they turned down the blacktop driveway to Sunny Groves. Her mother's anxiety and frustration was palpable, thickening the air like fog as they pulled off the rough edge of the driveway, the suspension jarred as the car rocked over shallow potholes. And then they were at the little slip in the back lot where Patrick's trailer had been inexorably parked.

Long morning shadows stretched across the park and left cold pools of air in the shade. Moisture beaded on the sides of the trailers and on the small gardens a few of the residents kept. The park felt empty as her mother ratcheted up the parking break in front of slip 19 and crossed the narrow patch of Astro Turf to the front door, visibly uncomfortable. Selena took the keys from her pocket. The lock was sticky, and by the time she finally got it opened it was like cracking the seal on an ancient tomb. The air was heavy with the ammonia smell of cat urine left too long in an enclosed space and stale cigarettes. The trailer was dim and claustrophobic as she drew back the curtains and looked to where mold flecked dishes were piled high in the sink.

"It'd be better to just burn the whole darn thing down."

"If you don't want to help me, I'll clean it myself," Selena said.

"It's filthy."

"Mother."

Almost immediately it was clear that the modest amount of cleaning supplies that they'd wedged in between the clothes and boxes of books weren't going to be enough to properly clean the place, but they set to work anyways emptying the narrow closets of Patrick's moldering clothes and working their way through the kitchen, throwing away or donating several times as much as they kept. In a far corner of the trailer – if there was such a thing – just behind the driver's seat, was an overflowing cat box, which was the only evidence of Patrick's once famous tomcat. As her mother worked in the kitchen, Selena, needing some distance, set to work in the bedroom. By noon there were half a dozen large garbage bags clustered outside the front door of the trailer, and it still seemed as though they'd barely scratched the surface. They made several trips across the park to the dumpsters, thudding the heavy trash bags into the metal bins with the finality of punctuation.

"Let's get out of here for a bit," Selena said, "and grab some lunch."

As they went to leave, Selena propped the door opened with an old brick.

"You're going to leave the door opened?"

Selena nodded.

"What about animals? Couldn't some animal get in there?"

"And what, trash the place?"

The following weekend, Selena's father came down and helped her strip the carpet down to the raw plywood beneath. Together the two of them replaced it with thin indoor carpet from the hardware store, working in a comfortable silence only broken by intermittent instructions as they cut along the grain with Exacto knives, leaving frayed fibers everywhere in their wake. It was easier to work with her father, who simply attacked one project at a time, focused and businesslike. The knife rasped and stuttered along the nap of the carpet; she flung narrow scraps out the door onto the Astroturf. By the end of the weekend, she had salvaged only one of Patrick's faded Carhartt jackets (several sizes too big for her), a dented aluminum tea kettle, and a box of paper backs.

That first night in the trailer was cramped but comfortable: a cocoon of growing familiarity. She set the pot to boil and pulled the paperbacks from their worn cardboard box one at a time, wondering if Patrick had ever done anything other than drink and smoke and read. Perhaps these were the only friends that he couldn't alienate no matter how hard he tried. It would be silly to look down on a Patrick for how he chose to live. After all, hadn't he chosen to live that way? Maybe it was true that she would have to walk a mile in Patrick's shoes to really understand who the man had been. Or, at least she would live in the home that had been his.

Taking a few paperbacks with her, she sat in the large captain's chair of the driver's seat, her legs draped over the arm, and started thumbing books whose titles she had heard of but never read. It occurred to her then that the cool silence belonged to her; the entire trailer belonged to her.

Outside, the clouds were a canvas for various gradients of amber until the shadows melted into a dark blue and the first stars appeared. A breeze buffeted the trailer, making it sway like a ship at sea. Selena walked outside then with her tea and stood shivering and thinking about her first night as a semi-official resident of Sunny Groves Trailer Park. The air was cooler there than it had been at her parents' house further down in the valley – perhaps because there were fewer trees to interrupt the persistent monologue of wind. She turned to go back inside when she noticed someone sitting on top of the Airstream several trailers away on the opposite side of the road. It was little more than a romantic silhouette, and she caught the faint scent of cigarette smoke as she turned and headed back inside.

As it turns out, the bus ride from Sunny Groves to the Red Apple is shorter than it had been from her parents' house. And, in the high arid heat of summer, she is grateful for the advantage. Once the hot, oppressive summer has settled in around May, both the buses and her trailer become mobile ovens. As soon as she returns home, she strips off her polyester pants and bright red polo shirt and hangs her apron on the back of the closet door, the plastic nametag still dangling from the breast pocket. Then she showers and changes into shorts and a T-shirt and steps out into the shade of the trailer onto the little square of Astro Turf that served as Patrick's lawn, pock-marked with cigarette burn constellations and threadbare where Patrick's forever shuffling feet gouged the plastic fibers from the thin fabric beneath.

There, on the thin patch of fake grass, reclining in a plastic Adirondack chair, Selena begins to think of the area in front of the trailer as something like her living room. Beer in hand and Patrick's old jacket draped over the back of the chair, she thumbs to the dog-eared page in *Treasure Island* that marks her spot. She is caught in the rush of feet on deck and the sea spray and Master Hawkins. The glare of the Airstream's metal siding creates inverted shadows on the road and interrupts her precarious thoughts. In an attempt to ignore the glare and heat, she tries to refocus on the page. The Airstream door bangs open and a rangy young man emerges. As far as she can tell he is about her age, wearing a short-sleeved shirt unbuttoned over his bare torso; a green and white trucker cap lets a fringe of greasy hair splay over his ears. For a moment or two she watches as this stranger lopes down to the side of the trailer and sets about removing the dust cover from a dirt bike. He does it in stages, so the yellow paint of the bike slowly emerges. Tossing the cover aside, he squats beside the thing and lights a cigarette, cupping his hands as he clicks the lighter despite the stillness of the late afternoon air. He stays on his hunches, near motionless, caught in meditation or contemplation. With an air of distraction, he rests his smoldering cigarette on the vinyl seat of his bike and disappears inside the trailer. In a minute or so he returns with a metal toolbox – bright red and sticker covered. He sets the box down and retrieves his cigarette, taking a long, deep draw and tilting his head back to exhale towards the sky.

Selena watches from her ad hoc living room, forgetting that she is not as invisible as she would like to be. She is in plain sight. If this young man would only turn he would see her, easily, sitting there, a mere twenty or thirty feet away in the half shade of her trailer. She watches him intermittently, trying to pick up the thread of the story, paging back and reading without truly comprehending the words: the words have become white noise. She is more interested in the metal on metal clatter of tools dropped into the box; the clatter a counterpoint to the ratcheting. The long afternoon goes on that way with the man tinkering with the bike and her watching him surreptitiously over the top of her novel. *It is only curiosity,* she tells herself. He is the type of person she would never have encountered had she never moved to the park. With some passing amusement, she realizes that they are probably the two youngest people in the whole park – at least the youngest that aren't living with parents, relatives, or middle-aged lovers.

Around seven, as the sky begins to darken, she slips into Patrick's jacket. The fabric, worn soft with washing and infused with sweat and stale cigarette smoke, envelopes her. She closes her eyes and thinks of him for a moment, trying to recall the gregarious uncle of her youth, the same man who had given her her first driving lesson when she was twelve. He had been drinking most of the day and she was spending the afternoon in the park with various cousins while her parents had already gone home. She remembers his exaggerated and cartoonish sly wink. She remembers the way that he laughed and whooped like a teenager as she lurched out of the park and down the road to the old corner store that has long since been demolished. When she opens her eyes, the mechanic is putting away his tools. She tells herself that she's not attracted to him because, if she was, she would have gone back into the trailer and put on something more appealing. Her faded sun dress maybe – the one that shows off her legs. Her honesty, she decides, warrants another beer.

The angle of the sun highlights curtains of dust left in the wake of the manager's white pickup as she steps back out into her living room; she has just enough time to raise her hand as he rumbles by, nodding in acknowledgment. Slouching back into her chair, she tries to remember the page that she was on. She tries to recall the specifics, but the story has become intangible. Once again, daydreams fog out the words on the page. She sets the book aside and nestles down further into the chair. The mechanic is just now pulling the dust cover back over the angled metal handle bars and returns to his RV.

She sits watching him and thinking about the park and the boundaries of the place. Not far away she can hear the cars passing on the highway, displacing air and distance as the mechanic's cigarette smoke hangs in the air like Patrick's last breath. The door to the Airstream bangs open again and the mechanic steps down onto the hard-packed earth. The sun is a soft bright yellow. It's the last bright light before dusk. Selena squints against the glare of his trailer and watches as he places his hands on his hips and leans backwards at what seems to be an improbable angle. For the first time he seems to notice her – looking at her the way an animal does when something suddenly attracts its attention; the look is not so much startled as it is curious. He pauses there for a moment staring at her and then comes sauntering across the road with a certain loping easiness. There is only the crunch of gavel beneath booted feet and then he is at the edge of her lawn.

"You must be Patrick's kid."

"Niece."

"Heard he passed," the mechanic says. "Sorry to hear about that."

"Wasn't your fault."

"I get that."

Selena nods, unsure what to say. This lanky, grease-smeared mechanic, stands a few feet away, his hands jammed in his pockets like a shy little boy. Part of her wants to see how long he will stand there, shuffling his feet in the gravel and stirring up puffs of dirt with his boot heels. He lets the butt of his cigarette fall and places his toe over it, grinding it down into the dust.

"Selena," she says finally.

"Marsh."

"What kind of name is that?"
"It's Marshall. Only person that calls me that is my mom, though."

"Nice to meet you Marsh."

"Likewise."

Selena pushes herself up in the Adirondack so that she is sitting more than lounging and gestures towards the empty chair beside her.

"Where you from, Marsh?"

"Originally? Colorado."

"Not much of a talker are you?"
"Guess not."

Silence settles between them as they sit in the Adirondack chairs sipping beer and gazing across the road at Marsh's trailer. The sun sinks lower and lower on the horizon. *He isn't bad looking,* she thinks. He has the type of ropey muscles that come only from hours of manual labor and when he takes his hat off and swipes his hand across his forehead, she can see that his hairline is already beginning to recede, extending his forehead high above his eyebrows, leaving only an isolated peninsula of hair.

As the wind kicks up Selena shivers further down into the old jacket and tugs at the zipper, thankful that the beer has given her a warm, pleasant feeling. It's only shortly after she hides a yawn in the sleeve of her jacket that Marsh stands and stretches, planting his hands on his hips and arching again at the same improbable angle she saw earlier.

"Well, Selena," he says, "I thank you for the beer."

For several days after that Marsh is conspicuously absent. Th\e sky becomes overcast, and she is relegated to reading in the captain's chair, intermittently pacing to the window to glance out and see if the motorcycle has returned.

She's gets up to place a bowl of recently bought cat food in her living room in hopes of coaxing the cat back, thinking that just because Patrick has died that's no reason to evict the cat. In fact, Selena likes the idea of having a cat there, curled up next to her as she sips her tea and works her way through the box of ragged paperbacks. It's a life that she's stepped into, a life that fits her as comfortably as pulling on perfectly worn jeans or one of her father's old sweatshirts.

It's near midnight when Marsh finally returns. It is the sound of the idling truck that wakes her and brings her to the window, feeling vulnerable and shy in her old T-shirt and underwear. She watches through the narrow gap in the blinds as the men ease Marsh's yellow bike down a makeshift ramp and setting it down beside the Airstream. Mud cakes the side of each of those unfamiliar parts that have names that are a foreign tongue to her. A man tosses an old duffle bag to Marsh and they shake hands briefly before the men climb back

into the pickup and dissolve up the road past
the Garner's trailer.

Returning from work the next day, she finds
Marsh out front with a bucket of soapy water,
rinsing the grime off of the bike. The bus had
dropped her off near the entrance to Sunny
Groves and she had paused briefly by the
caretaker's trailer to drop off her lot fee. The
woman, Sandy, was sitting there on the porch as
if waiting for Selena. She holds court over a
gossip magazine, a cigarette resting between
her fingers. She barely acknowledges Selena
before prophesying about which celebrity couple
is most likely to divorce within the next month.

"Smart money's on the silver-haired one who
married that young Latina. Do we call you
Latinas now?"

"Don't know," Selena says, acutely aware
that the woman has mistaken her for something
that she is not. "Lot fee."

Sandy takes the check, looking at her as if
confused for a moment, and then tucks it under
the edge of her ashtray to keep it from blowing
away.

"Well, whatever we're calling them now,
that's my guess. Put money on it."

Selena smiles politely and makes her way
down the road to her trailer. Her shoulders and
feet ache from the eight-hour shift standing

behind the register at the Red Apple. She's
noticed lately that she no longer has the energy
to smile at people and carry on polite chatter.
It's become a stretch – a chore. At first it had
seemed easy and comfortable. But now, she is
like those checkers that have been there for too
long – checkers who punch in the numbers for
various produce without having to consult the
cheat sheet taped in front of them. Even
bagging groceries has become an automatic
thing.

She is only twenty or thirty feet from him
before she looks up and see's Marsh. She slows
to watch him, knowing it is better than standing
and staring because he might take that the
wrong way, although she isn't certain what the
wrong way might be. Passing Marsh is like
passing an unfamiliar dog chained to a post. She
knows that she has to walk past him, but there
is a reluctance that makes her heart quicken
and steps slower. As she closes the distance, he
raises the sponge in acknowledgement,
seemingly oblivious to the water dribbling down
his forearm and dripping onto his jeans where it
leaves dark spatters along his thighs. She is
self-conscious of the ill-fitting black slacks and
the Red Apple apron, plastic nametag still
dangling from the sole pocket.

Mustering what self-restraint she has, she
manages to be nonchalant and confident as she

walks past, plastic grocery bags rattling in her hand. He barely looks up to see her. It's impossible to know if he notices or not. Within another dozen paces she is at her trailer. Door open and warm air greeting her in a thick wall, she enters. The door is barely closed behind her as she strips out of her clothes and steps into the shower, the water as cold as she can bear. Already this is a ritual; a cleansing away of the workday; a baptism into the second half of the day. A day she will be able to spend reading and drinking tea or taking the occasional walk around Sunny Groves, though the walk doesn't amount to much. She passes pink flamingoes and dogs chained to posts. A growing vocabulary: double-wide's and single-wide's, fifth wheels and Class C's. By the time she has showered and changed, Marsh is drying the bike with a tattered rag in smooth even circles. It's a gesture that smacks of affection. He pauses to inspect a nick in the paint, or squats to peer into the skeletal innards of the machine. Her first impulse was to sit in the Adirondack and watch him from a distance, but something in her told her that all things being fair, it was her turn to make the short walk over to his trailer.

All the same, she pauses for a moment, tapping *Treasure Island* against her hip, before setting it on the chair and taking her sunglasses from the perch atop her head and running her fingers through her hair, hoping that it looks more tousled than carelessly messy. Would he care about such things? He's a mechanic living in a trailer park after all, and there must be a different standard here – no need to put on airs or live up to some sort of societal pretension. She thinks of the Garner's place on the corner, where the miniature plastic picket fence encloses an almost too cheerful yard with a bathtub garden and a collection of glinting glass fishing floats that catch the light, creating puddles of color in the dust. All of these things are signs that people no longer care what other people think; not laziness, exactly, or tackiness, but a shear confidence in self and personal preference. All of it, suddenly and inexplicably, reminds her of the flabby old women at the YMCA, who are shamelessly content to walk around the locker room stark naked. Her mother had told her that it is one of life's greatest ironies: that the young are most reluctant to show off what should be shown off and the old are not reluctant enough to show off what shouldn't be.

She commits to walking across the road, and he is looking up now, without much surprise, as if he's been expecting her. He squints into the sun and pulls himself to his feet and, for the first time, she notices that he is much taller than she had originally thought – perhaps a hair taller than her father.

"Looks like you had yourself some fun there, Marsh," she says.

Marsh glances at the bike and says, "Race last weekend."

"Figured it was just something you did for fun."

"Semi-pro, actually," he says as he wipes his still wet hands on his jeans. "You just finish work?"

She nods.

"And now?"
She shrugs.

"Come on, I'll take you for a ride."

"Never been on one of those before."

"Nothing to it," he says. "All you have to do is hold on."

Before she can say anything, he turns and heads towards the door of the Airstream, leaving her stuck there for a moment, uncertain. Is she supposed to follow him? And then he is coming back out of the trailer with a helmet in each hand, one angular and visored with the same bright Crayola yellow as his bike, the other is rounded and black. The latter he hands to her as he tugs his own helmet down and fastens the chin straps. The textured smoothness of the helmet is cool beneath her fingers.

"Right now?"

Marsh is already climbing onto the bike, walking it out towards the side of the gravel road.

"Think about it too much and you won't do it."

Selena sets her sunglasses on the window sill of Marsh's trailer and pulls on the helmet. It's as if she's been submerged – the sounds of the park are muffled by foam and Kevlar. She pushes up the plastic visor in order to hear him better, but he says nothing. She rests her hand on his sinewy shoulder, she kicks her leg over the bike and suddenly she is flooded with the irrevocable feeling of vulnerability. She sways with the bike as Marsh forces down the kick starter and the bike is suddenly a feral thing, guttering and whining beneath them.

"No turning back now," he hollers over the noise.

And he is right; it is too late to turn back as the tires turn dust and they merge onto the smooth blacktop of the highway.

The complete surrender of control as the road rushes past them inches below their feet is exhilarating: the insulated sounds and road noise and the cars whisking by in her periphery and even the sun have never appeared quite the same way since seeing it through the scratched plastic of the visor. Then there is the wind. The sharp and bitter sting prickling her skin, raising goosebumps. Her skin remembers that only a dozen minutes ago it was warm to the point of tanning to the deep chestnut brown she knows she can gain. They are cresting the top of the hill and Sunny Groves is reemerging, laid out below them like some sort of diorama of pastoral Middle America: the rows and columns of evenly spaced trailers and somewhere in the back corner, the sun is glinting off of Marsh's Airstream and the windows of the double-wides facing the highway reflect the blacktop. There is the click and change in pitch as Marsh downshifts. Her hands and arms, once pinpricked by the wind with goose bumps, are heating up as the wind slackens and the heat returns. Marsh makes a wide, graceful turn back into the park. Sandy glances up from her magazine and waves; Selena wants desperately to wave back but can't bring herself to pull her arms from their bear hug around Marsh's waist.

As they ease into the park, Selena realizes that this is why boys buy motorcycles. It's why they learn to play guitar or get tattoos or smoke. The reason is altogether different from the reason they learn to throw a perfect slider or play poker.

Marsh slows to a stop in front of the trailer and plants his feet firmly on the ground on either side of the bike, nodding over his shoulder to her. She steps off the bike now, as awkwardly as she had gotten on, her legs still shaking from the confluence of cold and excitement. She steps back and removes her helmet as Marsh walks the bike backwards towards the trailer before cutting the engine and rocking the bike back on its kickstand. She can feel herself grinning as he unsnaps his helmet and yanks it off, smoothing back his sweat drenched hair, highlighting his widow's peak.

"You're smiling," he says as he takes her helmet.

"Guess I am."

"Knew you'd like it."

"Guess I owe you a beer."

"Guess I'd take one."

The bike ride does not immediately change things between them. Eventually she'll realize that the ride was the catalyst that diverted friendship towards romance. She can tell that there is, what her mother would call, "chemistry" between them. As much as she thinks about sleeping with him, she relishes that chemistry – the electric feeling- that courses through her shoulders. She basks in the glow of wanting and being wanted.

Originally, Selena had thought of Marsh as shy and reserved, but soon discovered he was only slow to warm up. Once warmed up, however, he was plenty talkative and had the dry wit of someone who liked to see other people struggle to decide whether or not he was joking.

Before long, the two of them are spending Thursday nights down at the casino, where the other bikers hang out. The driver of the white pickup, Dave, works at the same auto parts store as Marsh and the two of them had grown up together. And then there were a handful of others: bikers, mechanics, and construction workers. All of them enthusiastic as puppyish teenagers about anything that accelerates quickly. While some of the boys drift off to gamble, Marsh admits that he has given up gambling on account of not being very good at it.

"I'm a full throttle person," Marsh says.

"He means that he's too aggressive at the poker table," Dave explains. "I mean, don't get me wrong, He's aggressive on the course, too, but it makes sense on the course. You have to be aggressive. Poker is a thinking man's game. A patient man's game."

"Racing is a game of patience."

"It's not about the split-second decisions and opening the throttle up. When it comes to gambling, Marsh is a one pump chump. I hear that you can tell a lot about the way a man makes love by the way he gambles."

"Thanks, bud," Marsh says.

"No problem."

As Marsh hangs his head in mock humiliation, Dave wonders off a bit unsteadily to find the others. The two of them quickly becoming the gravitational center for the others: for an hour or so at a time they are alone, drinking at the bar, and then one of the other guys will show up and order a beer and a shot and hang out for a moment before slowly slipping out of their orbit.

For weeks things move slowly. Selena spends her shifts at the Red Apple with a renewed sense of friendliness and a hint of distractibility as she's given to glance out the front windows of the market any time she hears a motorcycle revving down the road. Weekends, the two of them might sit in her small yard drinking and talking. It's how she finally learns that he scrimped and saved for years in Colorado, working as a construction worker during the days and as a dishwasher nights and weekends. His parents thought he was saving for college. He could live at home, they said, start at community college and transfer to CU Boulder.

It took the better part of the year to save enough to buy the trailer. The night he explained to his parents that he was going to travel was one of the worst of his life. There'd been yelling. Accusations of ungratefulness. Once in a Blue Moon, he says, he gives them a call, but they never talk long.

It's somewhere during one of those long afternoon conversations that they end up having sex in Selena's trailer. The sex is average, which is what she likes most about it: the slow, predictability of almost boring sex on her unmade bed, without the whips and chains or other things she might have anticipated from a biker living in a trailer park. Afterwards, as they lay in her bed, she inhales the combined smell of their sex and sweat and smiles to herself as she examines the cartoon dog tattooed on his chest. A small and faded thing, slowly being overgrown by his patchy chest hair.

"This is my favorite," she says as she runs her finger along his clavicle to the hollow beneath his Adam's apple.

"Broke it twice."

Selena twists in bed, rolling onto her hip and propping herself up on one elbow. Looking more closely she can make out a jagged lightning bolt of a scar, faint and pale where it transverses the bone.

"Few years ago, I broke it during a race. Hurt like hell. Blood. Bone through the skin. Broke it again during a qualifying race a couple years later."

"Guess I didn't realize how dangerous racing could be."

"That's right," Marsh says. "You're dating a dangerous man."

"Who said we were dating? Besides. Maybe it's not that you're so much dangerous as you're accident prone."

Selena can't pinpoint the exact reason she decides not to introduce Marsh to her parents. Although, she knows that it has something to do with the sacredness of this: her first adult relationship. Before moving to the Park her parents had, inevitably, met whoever she was dating. Those first skinny boys on bicycles; boys who smelled of sweat and bubble gum. Boys whose furtive kisses were sweat and almost naïve. Then it was the overly eager teenage boys in hand-me-down cars or borrowed sedans too sensible to be cool. Even as an adult she felt guilty for having boys her own age – boys who were barely men – down into her little basement room.

A true sense of independence, she realizes, requires remarkably little: a battered Winnebago haunted by stale cigarette smoke and mildew. It is only a trailer, but it is hers and that part is the most vital. She could drink during the day and have Marsh over for modest, if not slightly too loud, sex in her trailer knowing that the whole thing was rocking on worn out suspension, an unabashed announcement to anyone who hadn't already guessed as much. If it matters at all, it's only because the whole thing is hers. She is her own woman now, free from parental oversight, and existing in her own space. The trailer is hers. The experience belongs only to her and Marsh, all of which seems absolutely fine with him. He has no interest in meeting her parents. Though only a few years older, he had already begun to adopt an air of superiority – a faux wisdom that cropped up in his repeated aphorisms. No one, he liked to say, could learn how to exist for themselves until they learned to live on their own.

The mud and dirt course where Marsh often races is twenty minutes away in Banner City. Everything about the course seems barbaric and grizzly. The earth sculpted into high ramparts scored by thin, knobby dirt bike tires. Hay bales and rusting chain-link encircles the course. Rooster tails of mud dog the riders as they lean into the curves, their machines stubbornly defying gravity until one or two of them inevitably skids into each other or collides with the hay bales. In his bright Crayola yellow leathers, Marsh and his bike melt into an angry, exhaust coughing wasp as he cuts precariously around and past other racers. Selena clusters with the other girlfriends and friends in the aluminum stands near the finish line, their feet chiming staccato rhythms as they hop and stamp in encouragement. On race days, this cacophony becomes fevered. Selena finds it bizarre though since none of their shouting or clanging could possibly penetrate through the din of engine roars. But that doesn't stop her from joining in.

However, today is not a race, but a qualifier. Selena holds her breath as he nears the end of the final lap, glancing up at the official clock as the numbers tumble past. He zips past them, the clock stops. It's an excellent time. His helmeted head swivels towards the clock as the bike begins to coast and he throws his hands triumphantly in the air. She reminds herself to exhale.

As he stands there beside the bike and kisses Selena, she insists that they organize a celebration back at the Park. She wants to celebrate this with him. She knows how important it is to him, and she has begun to think of the others as their new family. This is the thing that separates her from her parents – as Marsh has said – and the thing that brings them closer together. It's the gray area between summer and fall. By the time Marsh shows up at the trailer, there are a handful of bikes parked there alongside the Airstream, and Dave has brought out a propane grill, which he stands in front of like a prize-winning chef, flipping burgers with an old spatula, beer in hand. Lawn chairs have been set up there, and they've dragged over the Adirondack's from Selena's place. By the time Marsh gets back Selena is already several beers in, and they toast heavy shots of tequila. She wants this all right now. She revels in the feeling of being the girlfriend of the victor, and she wonders if this is why the girls in high school had scrambled to date the quarterback of the football team.

The sun having set long ago and her vision blurring, she is vaguely aware that her world is beginning to tilt. The air is thick with cigarette smoke and laughter and jokes and curses, and she is losing track of the conversation. She sits in her Adirondack and watches Marsh and convinces herself that he is eying one of the other girls with a little too much interest; that they are flirting. From her slouched position, she tries to catch his attention, but he isn't looking at her.

And then she is pushing herself to her feet and walking unsteadily to where his bike is parked. The plan makes perfect sense. He will see her sitting on his bike and he will find her irresistible and come over to her. Perhaps they'll disappear inside his trailer, and the others will smile knowingly at each other. She is near the bike and then the world stutters and there is crashing and rolling. Someone is hauling her to her feet and she can hear people shouting. Marsh is there suddenly cursing and looking at his bike which is now – improbably – lying on its side. With Dave's help, Marsh is able to right the bike and he reaches down into the gravel and picks up one of the foot pegs which has somehow snapped off. He stares at it for a moment before cocking his arm and flings the piece of plastic and metal skyward over the trailer. He is smiling as he steps towards her. One of the other girls is holding her steady and brushing the dust from Selena's knees.

"Marsh," she says.

But the answer is not a kiss or a hug or an embrace. It's a well-aimed backhand that catches her below the eye and tears her from the

stranger's grip. Someone else – the same woman
maybe – is yelling at him as he leers at Selena.

Selena stands for a moment – eye stinging.
She can feel the pressure of tears behind her
eyes. For a moment, she had been on the top of
the world, and now she has tumbled far from it.
Everything is shattered. She turns towards her
trailer without saying anything. Behind her she
can hear Marsh calling out some sort of apology
and Dave's voice telling him to let her go. There
is silence from the other people that have
gathered there, and she knows that they are all
watching her as she reaches the door of her
trailer. As gracefully as she can manage, she
steps inside and closes the door behind her. For
the first time since she has moved to the park
she locks the door behind her. Still clothed, she
collapses into bed.

When she wakes in the morning her mouth
is a feral thing, the texture of sandpaper.
Overnight, the swelling in her cheek has
hemmed in her eye. The puffiness is dogged by
deep throbbing as Selena drags herself from bed
to shower, where she stands wincing as the hot
water streams down her face. She runs the
water until it is cold, gulping in great
mouthfuls. In the mirror, she can see that the
swelling is less insidious than the bruise that
has crawled beneath her eye like a yellow and

brown slug. She has doubts that she will be able to cover it with makeup. When she is dressed, her apron tied around her waist and nametag pinned to the pocket, she rests her sunglasses gingerly on her nose. At least the bruise will be hidden until she gets to work.

On the bus, Selena decides that she wants everyone to see her bruise. She wants the entire Market – the other checkers – to know what Marsh has done to her, especially the girls who had drooled over him the afternoon he had stopped to pick her up on his bike. But now they have the look of uncertainty and fear and sympathy as she enters the break room and places her sunglasses with her backpack in the small locker.

The bruise elevates her from nearly invisible checker to tourist attraction. Everyone seems to be asking her what happened to her eye. She starts out with honesty and ends up with lies. Everyone has heard the stories of abused women from the front page of newspapers and in the pages of celebrity magazines that Sandy reads.

At the end of work, she is tired and frustrated as she carts her plastic bag of aspirin and beer to the bus stop and stands there sweating in the direct sunlight, squinting even behind her sunglasses, the bruise throbbing richly.

She walks past Sandy, her sunglasses perched securely over the bruise. She does not want sympathy from her neighbors. She does not want them telling her what she should do next. She passes the Garners' place, half expecting to look up and see Marsh there tinkering with his bike. She is uncertain as to whether or not she wants to see him. She imagines confronting him with the bruise, shoving his nose in his own mess. But maybe being too tired to care is a blessing in disguise. So long as she doesn't cave in and forgive him, and she steels herself against that possibility. Maybe he would blame her or the drink or both of them. Maybe he would blame his own heightened emotions – but she tells herself that she must be strong, she has to remind herself that she cannot let him get away with this.

The bike is gone, which means Marsh is gone and she hopes and prays that it is some sort of guilt or embarrassment that has taken him away. She showers and changes and goes out to sit beneath the awning of her trailer as a light rain begins to scatter across the Park. As the air cools, she wraps herself in Patrick's faded Carhartt jacket.

It's as she's sitting there, thoughts creating a labyrinth of possibility and excuses and potential inoculation against Marsh's charm that she happens to hear Tom whistling as he makes his way up the gravel road. There he is, the broad-shouldered caretaker. He glances up and they exchange lazy acknowledgements, and he ducks beneath the awning. He pushes the hood of his rain jacket back from the hedge-like brush of thick white hair. This, Selena thinks, is a text book example of the phrase flat top. She thinks it looks as though one could balance a book perfectly on top of his head.

"You ought to work for the post office," he says.

"Sorry?"
"Rain or shine. You're always out here. You know the motto, 'neither snow nor rain nor heat nor gloom of the night something something appointed rounds.'"

He steps closer and points to her sunglasses. His paternal strength makes her feel obligated to take them off, which elicits a low whistle from this almost stranger.

"That's quite the shiner."

Selena rests her sunglasses on her nose again and gestures to the empty chair beside her.

"Handiwork of Mr. Airstream? If you're interested, he left early this morning. I'm guessing that has something to do with your souvenir."

For a long moment, they sit there as the rain picks up into a chattering staccato. It cuts at a low angle, soaking the edge of the Astroturf. Tom steeples his hands but doesn't look at her.

"I'd be happy to talk to him, if you like. I know it's not my business. You can handle yourself."

"It's fine," she says.

"Saw a lot of this on domestic violence calls back in the day. But I imagined you'd want to take care of this. Change your mind, you know where to find us. Sandy's going to be pissed as hell at that boy."

As she begins to process his words and the thought that a complete stranger would be angry on her behalf, Tom stands and pulls his hood up. He gives a slight wave and disappears up the road, glancing from side to side at the trailers as he walks. The loneliness that she is steeping in could easily be remedied with a call to her parents to have her mother come get her—but then Selena would have to explain everything, which for some reason seems tantamount to admitting that she is incapable of caring for herself. There would be judgment – regardless of how intentional or unintentional – even though they knew nothing about Marsh. They don't know life at Sunny Groves. They couldn't understand what it means to live on that island or what it is like to live in Patrick's place. Although she hates to admit it, it seems as though the only person that she has any deep and true understanding with is Marsh. Patrick would have been on that list, but he has long since been dead and gone.

Several days after he hit her, Marsh skulked back to his trailer. Although she hadn't heard it, his bike reappeared in the middle of the night, and stood beside his trailer like something newly planted. The glare off the windows is harsh, but she can tell that behind them the curtains are drawn, and she can imagine him in there, peering through a gap in the curtains. She imagines he is watching to see when she leaves so that he can feel comfortable enough to leave his own trailer. Days have passed but not enough of them for her to decide on any significant course of action. The swelling has gone down and a purple half-moon beneath her eye is the only relic that remains.

It's only by shear accident that she sees him one afternoon as she is on her way to work. Keys, muffled only slightly against her apron, rattle in her hand as she adjusts the strap of her backpack. Dimly she becomes aware that he is there, less than twenty yards away, leaning in the open doorway of his trailer. As soon as he sees her he steps down but misjudges the steps and stumbles for his balance. She isn't sure if she's afraid he'll hit her, or if she's afraid he'll kiss her. She slows and stops and then he is in front of her.

"Jesus," Marsh says.

"You should have seen it a few days ago."

"I had no idea."

"You'd have been proud of yourself."

"Shit. I had no idea."

She imagines moving towards him, wrapping her arms around his waist and breathing in oil and cigarette smoke and sweat. He seems restless now, and she can see that he is going to move – to do something – and she knows that she must do something first. She clutches her keys tighter in her hand.

"Fuck you, Marsh."

She turns back to her trailer before she even considers it. She is late for work, but she no longer cares. She will call in sick. Once back inside with the door shut and locked, she can hear him outside of her trailer calling her name. It isn't so much as yelling as it is a monotonous repetition until it begins to sound like a lowing chant. After several minutes, he falls silent and she hopes he has finally walked away. When she peeks out the window, she sees Tom standing near an overly and uncharacteristically animated Marsh. Tom for his part has the expression of a parent amused by the limp protests of a toddler. Finally, Marsh turns and walks back to his trailer. Whatever they say is lost to the Styrofoam sandwiched between the Winnebago's vinyl shell and faux wood paneling.

She knows that when there is a knock at her door a moment later it's Tom, and she swipes at her eyes with the back of her hand– there is still pressure heavy against the backs of her eyes. She clenches her jaw and looks skyward, gathering her breath before opening the door.

"We'd like to invite you over for dinner tonight," he says. "What time's good?"

"That's kind of you – "

"Sandy isn't about to take no for an answer."

She passes Tom and Sandy's trailer as nonchalantly as possible and makes her way towards where her own trailer is on the far side of the park, a quarter mile off. The air inside the trailer is warm and close, as humid as a jungle. Relishing in the cool water, Selena showers and changes into a flannel shirt worn thin by a thousand washings and a pair of jean shorts. She'd wandered up and down the aisles of the Red Apple trying to decide what might represent a reasonable contribution. Each step down an aisle was a step through familiar territory and a miniature prayer for inspiration.

In the end, she'd settled on a bag of chips and a six-pack of beer. Yet, as she makes her way across the park, hair hanging luxuriously damp against her neck, she is self-conscious. She should have bought something else.

Feeling waifish, she steps up onto the deck that Tom has no doubt built by hand. The treated boards lay perfectly even and flush together, and everything about the place is crisp and orderly. Even the herbs in their plastic flower box seem to be growing with fairy-tailish obedience. Before reaching the last step, Sandy is already pushing open the screen door.

"Evening dear," Sandy says, cocking her head to examine the bruise beneath Selena's eye. "You'll live. Gives you a tough look. Like that lady in the boxing movie."

Selena hugs the older woman awkwardly, but the embrace is motherly and reassuring. She is acutely aware of the cans rattling against each other and the crinkle of the plastic bag of chips. She holds the offerings out in embarrassment and Sandy laughs good-naturedly.

"Let me find some salsa."

She sits looking at these strangers and eats the barbecued ribs and baked potato in front of her. They are old enough to be her

grandparents. Neither of them has mentioned
Patrick, and she wonders if they knew him and
how well they might have known him. Was
there some sort of deathbed request that he
made, begging them to look after her? The
cinematic appeal plays out into morbid fantasy.
Perhaps, here in the park only twenty miles
from where she grew up, she's found an island
that is farther away from home than any place
she could have reached geographically. Yet, she
knows it's only temporary.

In the Comfort of Memory

After Nancy leaves from work, Paul wheels
around the kitchen stacking the breakfast
dishes in the drying rack and setting the coffee
to percolate. He's never been one for routine
except for clearing away the dishes and having
his morning cup of coffee. Aversion to routine
was a habit the Navy failed to break him of, and
now, as he sits in front of the kitchen window
waiting for the coffee to boil, he notices that the
bird feeder on the porch is empty.

Late mornings are his. The radio murmurs
from the kitchen counter as he wheels down the
hall to carve. Arranged on the leather desk
blotter are a variety of tools gathered over a
decade. Knives and chisels lined up evenly in
neat rows. Clusters of paint in crumpled tubes.
An old shoebox full of sandpaper of varying grit,
worn bare along creases and torn ragged at the
edges. A half dozen projects sit in various stages
of completion. Whether he paints or carves is a
matter of whim. Right now, he wants to hear
the rhythmic rasp of paper on wood as he
progresses through varying grits of sandpaper,
smoothing the wood until it has a downy
smoothness.

In the faint lull of morning he loses track of
his thoughts and allows the minutes to drift

past as he sets to work. And so, he has no way of pinpointing exactly what he was thinking about when the phone rings. He reaches the kitchen phone by the sixth ring.

"Mom's had a stroke."

No perfunctory hello. No warning. It's his sister's voice on the other end of the phone. He imagines Sophie sitting in her kitchen five hundred miles away in Butte.

"Is she alive?"

"I'm headed to the hospital now."

Paul watches as a lone starling eases up and perches on the narrow plastic ledge of the feeder.

"Nancy has the car," he says. "We'll be there as soon as we can."

Paul scribbles the address on the pad of paper by the phone and circles it. He will look up directions as soon as gets off the phone, to be sure, but he has an idea of where the hospital is.

"Is Carl with you?"

"He'll meet me at the hospital."

And then he is alone again in the kitchen. The hollow half-sound of the radio permeates the incongruous stillness of the house. As he plugs the address into the computer he tries to recall the last conversation he had with his mother. He tries to remember what she looks like. *How strange,* he thinks, *that you can know someone your entire life and be suddenly unable to recall the curvature of their cheek or the angle of their chin.*

He lays his hand on the phone again. Hesitates. Picks up the receiver and puts it down again. Even now, midway through her shift at the Dental Clinic, Nancy must be whisking about the office in her mint green pajama outfit. This reality will catch up with her. He will wait for her to get home and tell her in person. This, he tells himself, is because Nancy has always been fond of his mother.

Paul returns to his desk. Spirals of wood cluster in piles. He picks up the piece again, a cartoonish golfer with a pot belly. Turning the figure over in his hands, he can feel the knurls and ridges of a thing incomplete. A part of him hopes that this will erase everything. *Ignorance is bliss,* he tells himself, *or something damn close to it.* No. There is no room for ignorance now; the morning has been irrevocably disrupted. He pauses in the hallway without direction or plan and tries to decide on a course of action. It should be easy to cope with this sort of abrupt change, but it's too far outside what he would have ever expected. It's too far outside what he could have imagined. He rocks his chair backwards and forwards, backwards and forewords, moving by minute increments, caught in the middle of indecision. The only recourse is to begin packing, which begins as a haphazard gathering of things. He retrieves their suitcases from the hall closet and stacks them on his lap and takes them into the bedroom where he has heaved them up onto the bed. He ferries clothing from closet to bed. Deliberates. Will he need something more than jeans and T-shirts? He alternates between placing clothes in the suitcases and removing them.

His memories of his mother, like his memories of walking, have long since faded; they have become amorphous and intangible things. To some degree, he knows, the memories have faded because he has allowed them to. As a matter of survival, he has allowed that last day to fade from him, the color draining out of it as he compartmentalized past and present. It had become necessary to divorce himself from that reality in order to preserve his own sanity. Yet now, despite years of sublimation, the memory resurfaces, gathering pigmentation – accreting into its own reality.

Suddenly, Paul is placing one foot in front of the other on the exposed slats of the roof and making his way to the chimney where the sun is sharp and garish against the aluminum flashing. Somewhere between one step and the next, his brain skips and he is awake again to the pain and debris and people yelling. The foreman is kneeling beside him, panic thick in his eyes, even as he tells Paul that everything is going to be all right. Paul can still feel the man's fingers at the back of his neck as he cradles Paul's head, an action far too intimate. Blood is thick in Paul's mouth as he mumbles that he is just fine, he just needs to be helped to his feet.

"Stay put," the foreman says. "The bus is almost here."

As the caterwaul of the approaching sirens rises in pitch, he realizes the sirens are for him. His senses have become raw and animalistic, snagging on the smell of sawdust and broken pine. It's then that he notices the uncharacteristic silence. The sirens have stopped. The chunk chunk of nail-guns has stopped. The squeal of the saw has stopped.

It was days before he was lucid enough to understand that the two-story fall had shattered his lower vertebrate. L2-L5, the doctor explained; almost his entire lumbar. For the first few months - cocooned in physical therapy and lengthy evaluations - he had held out hope that he would recover. It was increasingly obvious that any control he had over his legs had deserted him.

Will his mother have these same thoughts? Will she think of her last moments of coherent speech? Surely she is asleep now, sedated and connected to a heart monitor and an IV. When she wakes will her thoughts come back to her, or will they remain tangled? His fear now is that she will be a living ghost. A vegetable. Or, worse, she will stare numbly and drool while complex and intricate thoughts gestate behind her eyes. He tries to envision his mother with the same type of complex speaking machine that is used by the scientist on TV. The stilted computer voice and brilliant thoughts irreconcilable with the man sitting motionless.

When he is done packing, he zippers the suitcases closed and stares at this first piece of evidence that things have irrevocably changed, but all he could think about was that the birdfeeder still needs to be refilled and that the trash should be taken out, and that a newly carved figurine needed to be sanded down. Paul is thankful for the mundane now. Those chores will occupy him, taking up space that would otherwise be penned in by his thoughts and frustrations.

It's after nine when Nancy gets home, but it only takes her one look at Paul to know that something is wrong. The front door hangs open behind her, creating an overly dramatic silhouette, backlit by an orange halo of streetlamp. Even as he explains the situation,

Nancy is already hustling to the bedroom, shedding her work clothes, which she tosses haphazardly on the bed. As she hoists her jeans to her waist and shimmies them up around her hips, he's silently urges her to move more quickly. Although there is no doubt from the way she moves that she is aware of the need to hurry.

Five minutes later they are out at the car and he is moving through the familiar process of transferring from chair to car. Paul scoots himself to the edge of the chair and lifts himself on to the board that waits there on the passenger side. By gripping the frame of the car, he can hoist himself across and settle himself in the passenger seat. Before long, they are following the highway east towards the place his sister owns in Butte. They are both simultaneously thinking and not thinking about the hospital. They don't talk about it as they steep in a silence that is tempered by the hush of road noise.

It is hours before they lay eyes on the hospital, and even when it appears, Paul must remind himself that somewhere deep inside that overly lit building his own mother is in a dim room attached to monitors and IVs. Perhaps – just now – a nurse has peeked into the room to check her status. She is scribbling something on her clipboard and clicking the pen closed and slipping it into her pocket. Visiting hours are over at the hospital, so they bypass it and continue east towards the house, stopping only for gas at a too-brightly-lit station just off the highway.

Never before has a simple stop for gas been so nerve-racking considering how long they have driven. He has waited too long to see his mother, growing increasingly worried that her situation might have worsened in the interim. It's that particular uncertainty that vibrates against his skin in the cloying static of the night.

It takes another ten minutes to reach his sister's house from the gas station. When they finally arrive, Carl meets them in the driveway and helps them carry their things into the house. They can smell something cooking as soon as they enter the house – a particular smell that must be the handiwork of his sister, who, like him, cooks without following a recipe. It's the way that their mother had taught them.

"Sophie just got home. Stayed until visiting hours were up."

"I'm sure she stayed as long as they let her," Paul says.

Sophie appears at the end of the hall, wiping her hands on the edge of her apron. She has taken on a gaunt look. Even her smile betrays her utter exhaustion. When she reaches them, she leans down and kisses her brother's cheek before giving him a tight hug and turns to do the same with Nancy. They are caught there – for the moment – in the other room a TV cycles through sports highlights and overly enthusiastic commercials for household cleaners. Somewhere beneath all of this is the high rush of the kitchen fan.

"I don't know what to say," Nancy says finally.

"Not much to say."

Paul follows her through the kitchen into the living room, where she sinks into an overstuffed loveseat. In turns, they each begin to say something but lose momentum after a handful of syllables until it finally gutters and burns out. The conversation picks up elsewhere. It's discomfiting how quickly conversation can drift to things like work and household chores even in the midst of hardship – but life will continue as it always has. That they know for sure.

Before the accident, Paul avoided doctors as much as possible, squeaking by with the occasional physical, and largely disregarding professionally doled out advice to eat healthier and exercise more regularly. Now, he no longer dreads hospitals in the same way that he once did – a side effect of too much time spent in the neutral colors of hospital hallways. Too much time spent wheeling over polished linoleum that no longer radiates the same sort of sadness and frustration it once had. For him, doctor visits are no different than having the oil changed in his car. In fact, Paul feels a sense of freedom because hospitals seem tailored to his wheelchair: wide hallways, deep elevators made to accommodate gurneys. e He doesn't have to shrink to pass through the doors–a result which makes absolutely the hospital far less claustrophobic than any other place – including his own home. Here, no one has ever looked at him with sidelong glances or pretended that nothing is different about him. Being in a hospital is the only place where he feels almost invisible – as though he could walk again.

Paul wheels himself down the unfamiliarly familiar hallway, the others trailing behind him like fond puppies. When they reach the right room, they pause for a moment and Paul waits as the others pass by him, their air of solemnity magnified. Their mother is sleeping, her head placed evenly in the middle of the pillow, the sheets stark and white and pure. It's as if everything has been created simply for their experience of this room. And now, as they take

turns kissing her slack cheek; a tall, willowy
nurse enters and goes about the business of
checking her IV. Their mother, he says, has
been lucid a few times since she arrived, but
hasn't been able to communicate very well.

"She's more or less out of the woods," the
nurse says, breaking what he knows is standard
protocol. "It'll be mostly rehab from here on
out."

It's a familiar refrain, one that has echoed in
Paul's mind until he was finally defeated by the
reality of his own situation – and he can't help
but doubt the advice and wisdom of health
professionals. This is territory that he knows
inside and out: the seeming inexorable visits
and therapy, prognoses that seem to become a
moving target. For Paul, it meant a brand new
normal, but their mother will adapt as he
adapted. Life goes on.

On the third floor of the hospital is a
cafeteria so small that it could barely be
considered a café. From their small table they
can hear the people in the kitchen arguing and
laughing – understandably and necessarily
disconnected from what the four of them are
feeling. It foists upon them the acknowledgment
that the world continues without them.

Inevitably, the conversation traverses an orbit that centers on their mother – but that orbit is forever widening, and now they have almost forgotten why they are there. Every time Paul realizes that they have moved away from the topic of their mother there is a heavy draw of guilt on his heart. It's while they are there that it's finally decided that the men will head to their mother's condo to see what they can do to get things organized.

"She's not going to be going home any time soon," Carl says.

Surely, regardless of the actual length of the hospital stay, she'll want some things from home: toiletries, clothes, personal articles. Besides, they will need to make sure that bills are being paid and that the trash has gone out. Neither Carl nor Paul is given to sitting around idle – it's a thing that makes them both irrevocably uncomfortable. It will be something for them to do. Something practical to occupy their time. And while they are out organizing things, the women will wait for their mother to awaken.

"She'll stay with us," Carl says. "Shouldn't take long to make the basement livable."

Carl drives Nancy's car – it's easier this way – primarily because Paul is well practiced at sliding in and out of their own vehicle. There isn't much to talk about since Carl already knows the way to the condo. As he drives, Paul marks the familiarity of the small stores and apartment buildings. There are plenty of things that have remained the same, and he can mark their progress based on the various landmarks. The drive across town takes about twenty minutes with traffic, and soon enough they are pulling into the lot of the complex where, on the second floor of the incongruous stucco job, is their mother's condo.

In his mother's condo, Paul tries again, consciously albeit unsuccessfully, to evoke his mother's face, but all he can remember is her face as he saw it that moment in the hospital. The last thing that he wants is a lasting mental image of her tainted by tragedy. In the kitchen, just down the hall, he can hear Carl gathering up the garbage and recycling. The door bangs open and shut as Carl carries the refuse across the parking lot to the dumpsters. The idea was to focus exclusively on the pragmatic, and Paul has digressed from that now by looking through the various photo albums that are stacked beneath the coffee table. He stacks several albums on the couch and then moves down the hall to the bathroom, where he barely looks at the labels of the bottles as he scoops the medicine into an overnight bag. Without much

thought, he gathers up his mother's toothbrush
and the things he knows she will want, whether
she knows it or not. For a moment, he wonders
if it would have been wiser to send the women to
the condo. At least they would have known
better what clothes to pack. Opening a dresser,
he is abruptly confronted with his mother's
underwear. He remembers when these things
used to hang on the clothing line in the
backyard of their one-story home in South
Dakota. But that is far away and long ago, and
then she had been even younger than he is now.
He has no idea of what she will want or need,
but he will take as much as he can.

The men stop by the house on the way back
to the hospital to drop off the things that they
have collected. Carl calls his mother-in-law's
landlord to make sure that the leasing company
knows what is going on. When he gets off the
phone, it is clear that there shouldn't be any
problems, and then the two men sit in the
kitchen sipping coffee.

Driving back to the hospital an hour later,
Carl prattles on about the practicality of selling
the condo. They are caught at stoplight after
stoplight, and he wonders if anything has
changed at the hospital, but he knows that if
anything had, either Nancy or Sophie would
have contacted him by now.

"You know," Paul says, "it does make sense. That is, selling the place. Do you think Sophie is willing to commit to taking care of her long term? It'd be a big thing to have her with you."

Carl drums his fingers on the steering wheel and, in the vacuum of silence, Paul begins to speak again.

"You're right, but, really, I can't imagine that there's some other way to go about it. She can't really be on her own, but we can play it by ear."

Carl, still drumming on the wheel, catches the even rhythm of the blinker and beats a staccato tattoo. The light turns and Carl eases the car around the corner. Paul can feel his pulse elevating. Carl is, in this situation, a borderline outsider. It's surprising that he should endeavor to broach such a subject and then remain silent on the part that actually matters. Carl may have been married to Sophie for fifteen years, but Paul is fifty-six, and has a good fifteen years on his brother-in-law. He is not mad at his brother in law. He's mad at the situation. He's mad at the truth, even though the truth is not something he can control. He wants to cling to the optimism that seems, minute by minute, to be siphoned away.

The second night they order take-out from a Chinese restaurant on 15th. As the driver passes the rustling bags to Carl, the two men argue about who will pay. In the end, Paul wins – after all they are the guests and it is only right that they should pay for the meal. They eat in silence; whatever conversation existed for the first two days has turned to mere vapor somewhere along the way as they shuttled from hospital to house and house to hospital. The chow mien and fried rice and egg rolls disappear, eventually the plates and boxes are empty and they no longer have anything to occupy themselves with – they no longer have any excuse to be together other than the obvious. And yet, they're all exhausted. They're exhausted from the trips back and forth across town, and they're exhausted from the emotional drain of trying to look strong for their mother and for each other. They are exhausted by the persistent uncertainty that hedges into pessimism and dogs any such recovery.

It's Paul that turns in first, excusing himself from the table and rinses his plate in the sink – refusing any help to do so. He faces little resistance. No one wants to say that he should or shouldn't be doing something. Everything has veered into hypersensitivity, perhaps a result of their frayed nerves. Now, as he lies in the unfamiliar bed staring at the unfamiliar ceiling,

he is thinking about – for some reason – all of
the beds that he can remember having laid in.
He thinks back to the comfortable twin bed that
he had as a kid, the one that he remembers only
dimly as a safe haven. And he remembers the
bunk that he had in the Navy, his next bed
really, and the way that the humming
machinery of the ship seemed embryonic – the
womb of a giant metal beast and the amniotic
fluid of the Pacific or the Atlantic somewhere
just beyond the thin skin of the ship. Next, the
bed that he shared with Nancy shortly after
their marriage. A bed that he remembers dimly
at best. Somewhere along the way there had
been a new bed and he thinks of it now, trying
to recall it, even if he barely can. And then the
numerous anonymous hospital beds that could
be raised or lowered, eased forewords and
backwards, at the push of a button. Finally,
there is the bed that they have now – not
entirely unlike a hospital bed for all intents and
purposes. Two halves of a seemingly apparent
whole. The independence of the affair had been
a primary selling point for Paul, who had
thought it counter-intuitive at first. If they were
married, why would they want to sleep
separately? Separate beds conjured images of
1950s sitcoms, where mother-dearest and
father-dearest occupied beds separated by a
modest gap of several feet.

But now he waits, lying in the guest bedroom at his sister's house, thinking back, for some reason, about beds. And he knows that when Nancy finally decides to turn in, she will make her way down the hall and undress in the dimness of the room – the light filtering through the gauzy curtains. And then she will slink beneath the covers and curl against him. While she lays there, he will think about how their world together could be shattered in only a moment. As much as he hopes to continue to exist with her, he can't help but think of life without her.

Paul admits to himself that they will have to leave soon. It's unreasonable to think they can stay until she is out of the hospital – there is no knowing exactly when she will be discharged. And so, he will be a state and a half away when his mother is transported to her new home – her daughter's home really – perhaps wondering why she hasn't been able to go back to her condo. Perhaps she will sense that she can't go back. Perhaps she already knows.

Dreams of a Stranger

At a quarter to four, the woman from the day care calls to tell Travis that Rita hasn't been by to pick up Caleb yet. Rita's nearly an hour late at this point, but Travis is more apologetic than he is worried since there are a number of reasons that might have delayed Rita. Before he hangs up the phone, Travis is already gathering up the papers he has been grading – mediocre essays on the root cause of the First World War – and stuffing them into his leather satchel. When he tries Rita's phone it goes directly to voicemail. He tries the number several more times on the fifteen-minute drive from Kennedy High to the daycare.

As he pulls into the parking lot, he scans the unfamiliar minivans and SUVs for Rita's car, hoping that maybe she beat him there. He parks near the entrance. Inside, his eyes strain against the dimness of the building until the dappled light clears and he sees Caleb crouched by a low table fussing idly with a wooden puzzle. When Caleb sees Travis, he pushes himself to his feet and gathers up his backpack, swinging it back and forth so that it ricochets off one leg and back towards the other. Travis nods an embarrassed apology to the woman behind the desk, scribbling his name on the little clipboard kept there for, no doubt, some aspect of liability.

It's as they reach the car that Caleb finally breaks their somewhat sullen silence.

"Mom picks me up," Caleb says.

"I know buddy."

"Where is she?"
Travis lets the question slip into unanswered silence as he buckles his son into the car seat, but when he climbs in on the driver's side Caleb asks again.

"Did she forget about me?"
"She would never forget about you, buddy. She just had some chores to do. So, I'm picking you up today.

Rita has not returned his calls. He scours his memory for any reason that she would be missing. Not missing, he tells himself. She is somewhere. She hasn't simply gone missing like car keys go missing. Hadn't she mentioned something about spending the day down in Corpus Christi with her mom? If she isn't at the house by the time they get there, he'll give Dorothy a call in Corpus and then maybe try the Salon. He will approach this logically; there's no reason to panic. Yet, as he turns down the street into their preplanned suburb, he can see that her car isn't parked there in the driveway. Nestled in his car seat in the back, Caleb is thumbing through one of his picture books, and as Travis glances at his son in the rearview

mirror, panic begins to prickle the back of his
neck.

"You know what buddy? We're going to have
the house to ourselves for a bit. Mom will be
home a little bit later, so for now it'll be just us
guys. Sounds fun, right?"

"Sure."

The captured air conditioning inside their
small house is almost too cold on Travis's skin.
There's no note on the kitchen table. Down the
hall in their bedroom the closet doors are
hanging open, and he thinks now that he must
be right. She must have headed down to Corpus
earlier that morning. He shakes his head,
knowing with a certainty that he's forgotten. He
slips out of his tie and shirt and makes his way
into the kitchen where he begins fixing Caleb's
supper: tater tots and chicken fingers. He is
dimly aware that he has pulled the ketchup
from the refrigerator door and sets it on the
counter. Caleb has already plunked himself
down in front of the TV and is in the process of
crashing and re-crashing his Matchbox cars.
Once dinner has cooled enough, Travis allows
Caleb to sit on the living room floor in front of
the TV to eat. Rita would scold him for letting
the boy eat supper on the floor, but it seems
right, one of those little concessions he'll make
while she's away. As Caleb eats, Travis settles

into the couch and picks up grading papers where he left off.

It's near sunset when he finally tells Caleb to turn off the TV and brush his teeth and get ready for bed.

"When's mom coming home?"
"A few days, son, she went down to see Noni."

"So, you forgot to pick me up?"
"Daddy got busy, buddy, I'm sorry. I didn't mean to forget you."

"It's okay. Next time don't forget."

"I won't, buddy."

After Travis puts Caleb to bed, he sits at the kitchen table with the last of the essays and listens to the familiar murmur of the house: the humming of the refrigerator and the intermittent clicking of the air conditioner. He thinks about calling his wife again, but assumes, as usual, that she's left her charger plugged in beside the bed, and by now her battery has died. He'll call down to Corpus first thing in the morning. Trying to grade the essays now, he realizes, is futile. Slipping the last of the essays back into his satchel, he grabs a beer from the fridge and settles down in front of the TV. He wakes several hours later. The movie he had been watching has ended and is replaced with an infomercial for a complicated exercise machine which looks like a torture device that would confound most masochists. Clicking off the TV, he drags himself down the hall to the bedroom and falls into bed still clothed.

Travis wakes sometime after seven and stumbles down the hallway to check on Caleb, who's already crawled out of bed and is sitting on the floor with his Legos. He pauses there for a moment, watching his son. Hair sleep-tousled and pajamas crinkled, the boy mumbles quietly to himself as he pieces the brightly colored pieces together.

It isn't until Travis has showered and is opening the dresser for a clean shirt that he notices the picture frame on Rita's nightstand is empty. The glass catches the reflection of the overhead light. A scrap of torn paper is tucked into the edge of the frame. Here is Rita's familiar, looping handwriting, and only a one-word apology: "sorry." Travis's brain stutters as he tries to make sense of the missing picture and the scrap of paper. As far as he knows, there is nothing that Rita has to be sorry for. Even as he showers he still clings on to hope that perhaps she would be back by that afternoon. Talons of doubt dig into his shoulders. He dials Corpus, but Dorothy tells him that Rita isn't there and the plans were for next weekend.

"Everything all right, hun?"

"I'm a little confused is all," he says. "Rita isn't here."

"Where is she?"

"That's what I'm trying to figure out."

Rita isn't answering her phone he tells her, and he hasn't seen her since the morning before; and now Dorothy is worried as well. He can tell by her voice –something beneath the cheerful hue of her words that betrays rising concern.

"I'll be up to the house as soon as I can, hun. Should be by early morning; there's just a few things to look after."

At least she'll be there to help him with Caleb, he thinks, so that he can sort this whole thing out. He hasn't mentioned the slip of paper to Dorothy, and something in the back of his mind tells him that he's simply overreacting. For a moment, he considers calling back and telling Dorothy not to trouble herself, there must simply be some sort of misunderstanding or miscommunication, and the whole thing may be sorted out before she even makes it up to San Antonio. He sits for a moment on the side of the bed staring at the picture frame before taking a deep breath and calling the salon. He's seen the picture so many times that he's nearly forgotten it. It's her favorite. A picture of Travis and Caleb down at the beach in Corpus for Caleb's third birthday, almost three years ago. The salon tells him that Rita isn't scheduled until Monday. The receptionist – someone who he only knows by voice- asks him if everything's okay. He's already growing tired of the question.

Travis stands in the backyard as the evening sun creates peepholes in the acacia that line the yard. The trees are far taller now than they were when Travis and Rita first moved in. The wind picks up and rattles the branches in the trees, wavering the sun. He knows the house behind him; the modest place that may be simple, but it's theirs. They'd sweated as they signed the reams of paper to buy the place, and that night they'd made love in their old apartment. Both of them were slightly sure and happy to think that it was then that Caleb had been conceived, but he has no idea if she still thinks of those times – wherever she is. It dawns on him that he has been waiting to understand her as if there will be some sudden explanation or realization, but he knows now that it's impossible; it would be as impossible as understanding the dreams of a complete stranger.

The grass underfoot is brittle and sharp and yellow, and he remembers the long, dragged out arguments that they'd had about what to do with the backyard. Rita had been adamant that they dig a pool, but Travis demurred, nervous that a pool would only invite tragedy. The last argument about the pool had been just after Caleb was born, and Travis had looked at his son lying on his belly in the middle of the living room and envisioned only a breathless version; blue lips and closed eyes. He'd never been able to chase away the thought that a pool might kill his son.

As he stands on the lumpy lawn he realizes that he was wrong; the answer, if there is one, is in the shovel that he removes from the corner of the garage. The words "our son will be fine" become a mantra as he presses the shovel into the dry ground and flings the first shovelful across the yard, where it bangs against the fence. It's not long before Travis is sheened in sweat made gritty from the flying dirt. A cloud of dust swells around him and he pauses, mouthing the mantra as he tries to shake the feeling that he is a digging a grave.

Dorothy arrives early the next morning and hugs him so tightly he feels as though he might fall apart. Both are able to put on a good face for Caleb so as not to let on that something is wrong while they talk in the kitchen. Together, they formulate the semblance of a game plan: Dorothy will take Caleb to the toy store and

Travis will go talk with the police. As if summoned by the mention of the toy store, Caleb patters into the kitchen and climbs up onto his grandmother's lap.

"How long will you stay, Noni?"

"As long as I darn well please," she says.

Caleb ponders the wheels of the matchbox car clutched in his hand.

"I thought mommy was visiting you," he says.

They've forgotten the initial lie, but Dorothy covers for them explaining that mommy did come down to visit her, but mommy decided to stay a piece longer down in Corpus to visit some old school friends. Now, of course Noni couldn't very well leave the men folk alone up here in San Antonio to fend for themselves. Who knows what kind of trouble they might get into. Travis smiles and nods in silent thanks. Before long, Noni is whisking her only grandson off to the store to get into trouble of a different sort.

When they are gone, Travis drives down to the police station and explains the situation to the desk sergeant sitting behind a desk stacked with papers and clipboards and a mumbling radio. The officer asks him to wait, and it's nearly a half hour before another officer emerges from some secret depth of the station to take his statement. This officer reminds Travis of one of his students. He's a kid barely old enough to drink and has the crisp, clean-cut look of someone overly confident in his importance. Everything about him seems to exude over-calculated professionalism.

"You wanted to make a missing person report?"

Travis holds back the urge to correct the officer's grammar and says, "I'm not sure."

"Someone missing?"

"My wife."

The officer waits, anticipating a punch line for a joke that will never come. If circumstances were different, Travis thinks, he might have actually made a joke. The officer retrieves a small notebook from his breast pocket and takes his time flipping to a blank page and clicking open his pen.

"How long has she been missing, sir?"
"Two days. Since Friday."

"Any reason you might suspect foul play? Anything in your residence out of place? Sign of a struggle?"

"No. Nothing like that."

The officer makes steady eye contact with Travis.

"Had you been arguing sir, at the alleged time of her disappearance?"

"No more than usual couples, I imagine."

"Any history of mental illness? Any particular medication? Any strange behavior as of late?"

"No."

The officer scribbled something in his notebook and flips the cover closed. As they sit there looking at each other, the officer taps the notebook against the outside of his thigh.

"I'm afraid, sir, that there actually isn't much we can do. Your wife is an adult, and adults have the God given right to do as they please as long as they aren't breaking any laws. If we have no reason to suspect a law was broken – or that foul play was involved - then our hands are tied."

Travis notices the man's hands. Well-manicured and the deep tan that comes with spending hours working outside in the high Texas sun. Travis scrutinizes the digital wristwatch and the glinting wedding band, and wonders how old this officer really is. But if he's married, surely, he can sympathize.

"I thought maybe you could file a missing person report or something."

"I understand your concern, sir, I really do. But you have to understand that there's nothing that I can do here. If you want to pursue it further, I'd recommend a private detective. A

P.I. might be better suited to help you track down your missing wife."

When Travis returns from the police station it is early evening and Dorothy is sitting at the kitchen table, leafing through one of her ubiquitous glossy magazines. The dishes have been washed and stacked in the drying rack bedside the sink; the laundry has been washed and folded and sits in the basket on the opposite chair waiting to be put away. Travis can see the bright purples and pinks of his wife's clothes intermingled with his own. Clothing that will soon be tucked away into dressers and hung in the closet awaiting her return, as if that might be any moment.

"I put Caleb down," she says, closing her magazine and setting it on the table. Without asking, she gets up and retrieves the bourbon bottle from the shelf above the fridge and pours them each a stiff drink. They sit there at the table in relative silence as he glances surreptitiously at his mother in law. He has never felt close to her despite nearly decade of marriage and numerous trips back and forth from Corpus, but now she is the one anchor that he has in this world. There is something comforting about her; perhaps it's a maternal instinct that has kicked in as she waits and drinks, the ice-cubes snapping and popping as the alcohol burns into them.

"The police," he says, "can't do shit."

"Can't imagine there's much they can do when the person that happens to have gone missing is a full-grown woman."

"I don't understand."

"Only one person could explain, hun, but even she might not know herself."

Noni finishes her drink and asks him if he wants another, but he shakes his head. She glances out the kitchen window at the ever-expanding ditch in the back yard and says nothing about it. As she gathers up her magazine and places her hand lightly on his shoulder, he knows that she has let this go as simply one way to deal with the situation. Perhaps she has learned this from thirty or forty years of marriage. He thinks of his father-in-law now, a stoic man who never seems to betray emotion unless he is talking about football or hunting. He feels her hand slip from his shoulder and watches as she makes her way down the hallway to the small guest bedroom. Over the five short years that they have owned the house, that room has been many things: storage, office, playroom, and guest room. For a time, they talked about having another child, and even went so far as to discuss it with some seriousness, but it had been left unresolved, and now he wonders if the room will forever remain empty when Dorothy heads back to Corpus.

Travis opens the sliding door to the backyard, reveling in the sudden change in temperature; the juxtaposition of bright air conditioning pushing against him and the hot dry desert air. He sets his drink on the patch of aggregate concrete just outside the door and retrieves the shovel from where he left it planted in the dirt. Soon he is moving to the rhythmic chunk and smack of dirt as one shovelful after another is heaved across the yard. Fragments of sod look like wild and unkempt hair as clods begin to bury the azaleas that Rita planted along the fence. Even as his muscles begin to ache and tremble, he is thankful for the distraction. He is thankful even as the skin is peeled back from his palms, leaving a slick glove of blood that sticks to the wood. He persists until he is wobbling on the verge of collapse, his legs shaking, and finally plunges the shovel back into the earth.

Sunday morning Noni is up early and has Caleb dressed for church, which she knows Travis won't attend. Just as well since he knows that she will close her eyes and bow her head and utter a lengthy prayer for Rita. She'll leave Travis to do what he feels needs to be done because, come Monday, he'll be back in class. She's assured him that she'll stay through the week, and he wonders if her willingness to stay is because she feels culpable for her daughter's absence. Of course, she must feel guilt. Guilt he understands. Guilt is what he feels as he excavates his memory for the fossilized remains of why she might have left. Left her husband and son behind in their house with only a scrap of paper bearing a one-word apology.

When Caleb and Dorothy leave, Travis sits in front of the computer and begins combing through Rita's email, half expecting to find evidence of an affair or some indication that she had been planning to leave, but there's no trace. And now, as he turns to the bank records, he notices the withdrawal from the branch downtown – a withdrawal that must have been done in person, he realizes, because of the amount. Several thousand dollars, not quite a quarter of what they had in their savings. It isn't long before Travis is slipping on his shoes and grabbing his car keys and heading across town to the bank, wondering why he hadn't thought to check sooner. But the bank manager has no new information to give him. Travis stands in the middle of the parking lot, letting the sun bake him, wanting to be incinerated there on the spot. Wanting the heat to ground him in the reality of the present. It's then that he sees the Greyhound station down the block, a station that he has passed countless times without ever considering the anonymity of the people getting on and off the busses. In the long-term parking lot beside the station, Travis finds Rita's car where it might have easily sat for weeks or months before anyone thought anything of it.

Although he hasn't brought her car keys, he knows that there will be no telltale clues. Through the windows he can see there is nothing on the seats -- no receipts or crumpled notes from an erstwhile lover. He knows that all he'll find in the glove box is a small package of tissues and a box of stale red licorice. It makes even less sense to him now that she would have left the car here if she only wanted to get away. She might have easily driven miles and miles to Corpus or Dallas or anywhere else for that matter, but she stopped here at the Greyhound Station just down from the bank and less than twenty miles from their house. Was it a whim, he wonders, a thing that she did simply because the bus station was there within easy sight of the bank? Or was it a premeditated thing that she had planned that morning, perhaps even as he was kissing her goodbye and saying that he would see her later that evening when he got home from work?

The Greyhound station is cavernous except for the long banks of chairs that remind him of the Dallas Fort Worth airport. Airports, though, amass people that are frustrated and tired and impatient. Here everyone seems more or less resigned to the reality of nearly inexorable waiting. If there is a waiting room for purgatory, he thinks, it would be something like this.

Sitting behind thick Plexiglas, a ticket seller gazes abstractly at the endless drip of passengers. He is anxious as he waits, uncertain what to say to this complete stranger and hoping that she will understand and, at the very least, sympathize with him. It should be human nature that this woman will want to help him, but when he steps up to the window she barely looks at him as she asks him where he is headed.

"Actually, I wanted to see if you could help me. I need some information. My wife may have bought a ticket here a few days ago, Friday, I'm pretty sure, and I was wondering if you could tell me where she might have been headed."

The woman looks at him now, eyes narrowing towards suspicion.

"You don't want a ticket?"

"My wife bought a ticket here. I was just hoping you could tell me where to."

"You want to know where your wife went? I can't give out information on passengers, sir. If she bought a ticket here, then that's her own business. If you don't want to buy a ticket, then I'm going to have to ask you to step aside."

"There has to be something you can do. All I want is information. Is there someone else maybe that I could talk to? A manager or supervisor?"

The woman glowers and waves him aside as she picks up a phone, still eying Travis through the scratched Plexiglas. It's the better part of a half hour before a side door opens and a tall, heavyset man emerges with the same sort of poorly concealed condescension that the cop had worn. The man explains in as much feigned concern and understating that he can muster over his professional detachment, that there is nothing that he can do. It's policy. Non-negotiable. Travis has no choice but to leave defeated, struggling to figure out how he will be able to get her car back to the house before it's impounded or towed or stolen.

Travis calls the school on Monday morning to arrange a substitute. Theresa, the office assistant that answers the phone, asks if everything is okay and all he can say is that he has some family things to take care of. The absence of detail combined with the fact that he rarely misses a day of work has become grist for the rumor mill. By Wednesday everyone has been infected with some strain of curiosity. By Friday people learn that no one has seen Rita all week. He notices it first in the knowing and sympathetic smiles of the other teachers as he arrives in the small teachers' lounge and sets his sandwich and apple on the top shelf of the fridge. He notices it again as the students eye him and whisper behind their textbooks.

In fourth period American Government, he catches a student passing a note that purports that Rita has run off with her lesbian lover to Canada. He recognizes the handwriting almost immediately, and he can't blame her. These students know nothing about American Government, and even less about the world outside the school's doors. The thing that surprises him is that the student who penned the note, a junior named Annabel, is popular and well meaning. A student who never struck Travis as even remotely malicious, which means that there are probably even worse rumors circulating behind his back.

During lunch, he runs hundreds of copies for a flier about Rita. He carefully lists all of his information, including his personal phone number, which he knows is risky, but he has to take a chance. In a town like San Antonio, somebody must know something. The question is whether or not they are willing to share that information with him.

After school, Travis drives downtown to the strip mall and parks in front of the dry cleaners that sits nestled next to an almost non-descript private investigator's office. It was the first listing that came up in his search, and now he is there, parked in front of this building, wondering whose life he has stepped into.

Every dim expectation of a pretty blonde receptionist in a smoky office with a Murphy bed is dispelled as soon as Travis pulls up to the office. Inside, it is so sterile that it might have been empty – as lifeless as the neighboring real-estate office and dry cleaners. The receptionist is a thin black man whose veins stand out on his arms and the backs of his hands.

"I called ahead," Travis says. "I'm here to see Mr. Corbett."

The receptionist nods, hands Travis a clipboard of paperwork and a pen, and asks him to have a seat. As he flips through the dozen or so pages of paperwork, he stretches his mind to remember his wife's social security number and bank accounts and driver's license. The paperwork seems, if nothing else, incredibly thorough, and although he knows that he should be comforted. The burden diminishes. The reality admission of reality distances him exponentially from his wife as she is now – as if dead – reduced to numbers and dates and an all-points bulletin of information: height, weight, hair color, eye color. He's embarrassed by the scratch of pen on paper in the otherwise quiet office. It's as if each scratch is an admission of isolation, and he wonders how he must look to a private detective, who, like the cop and the manager at the Greyhound station, will wonder what Travis did to drive his wife away. There is no other recourse. He finishes the paperwork and hands the clipboard back to the receptionist who gives the pages a cursory glance before turning and sitting the thing on the edge of his desk. It's a casual movement; performed how many times a day? How many times a week? A month? How many peoples' lives trapped there on the pages beneath the spring-loaded clip.

Travis sits flipping through expired magazines that are stacked on the side table, turning the pages without really reading much more than the occasional headline. It's ten or fifteen minutes before Corbett calls his name from the front of the room. The man is slender and silver-haired, but his voice is thick and authoritative, with a handshake to match. The two men make their way towards the back of the small office where Corbett's desk is nestled behind a shoulder high partition, and he gestures for Travis to sit as he stands there behind his desk flipping through the pages with as much enthusiasm as the receptionist before finally setting the clipboard aside and looking Travis square in the eye. Behind the man hanging on the wall is a cowboy hat and an old repeater rifle mounted to a plaque.

"I've a pretty good record with things like this," Corbett says at last, "but – and I have to be completely frank with you – the most important thing for you to know is that at some point you're going to have to decide what it is that you want from this whole thing."

"I want my wife."

"I realize that. I do. It's something that you have to bear in mind, though, that she may not want to come back. So, you'll have to decide what you'll be willing to settle with. Will you be okay knowing only where she is? I know that her return to her usual place is the ideal, but don't think that things will go right back to what they used to be, because that's not how it works."

"You can find her, though?"
"Like I said, I've got a good record. There's not a lot to go on, from what I can tell, but we have some bits and pieces." Corbett returns to the clipboard. "The bus ticket's a start. Of course,

the other big thing here that you're going to
want to take into account is how much money
you're willing to spend. I may not be the
cheapest in town, but damned if I'm not the
best."

"I can come up with what you need," Travis
says.

In the insulated road hush of the car, Travis
commits to pillaging Caleb's college fund to pay
Corbett's fees. The only comfort is the dim
prospect that Corbett may actually be able to
find Rita. Even after the bank accounts are
depleted, he wonders now if Corbett will be
right. Maybe Rita won't want to come home.
Obviously, she has no desire to be found. There's
no breadcrumb trail to follow. What he knows is
this: even if Caleb's college fund is depleted,
they'll have answers.

Like a bad movie, he imagines a roadside
reunion. Rolling fields of wheat or corn and dust
in the air. Two cars parked facing each other
and the tension of a hostage exchange. Caleb is
not there. Corbett is standing in the middle
distance. What would be left to say?

A month after Rita's disappearance, the hole
in the backyard has grown deeper and the edges
have been squared into the rough shape of a
pool. The excavation has yielded large berms of

dirt that have built up along the fence. Although he knows that at some point he will have to call someone to come and install the pool, he will wait for now – there is solace in climbing down into the pit where the air is cool and damp. As he stands there in the bottom, barely able to see over the edge, he runs his hand along the rough walls of the pit, dirt crumbling under his touch and rattling to the ground. The calluses on his hand are now thick pads with skin peeling back from his palms in jagged pieces. Sour sweat and earth sting his hands as he pushes himself up out of the pit and rolls onto his back and stares up at the hollowed-out bowl of the night sky.

With school coming up on Spring Break, Travis knows that Dorothy will head back to Corpus again for a week or so. She's been a Godsend, and he has to acknowledge that she still has to live her own life, no matter how guilty or culpable she feels. As if to make up for this guilt, Noni has been running the laundry machine and stocking the cupboards with food; she's been like a one-woman force of nature, swirling through the rooms of the house. As he stands in the kitchen, he tries to think back to the less then pristine kitchen as it was before Rita left. The changes are, overall, subtle. The way that the kitchen towels are folded crisply over the handle of the oven where they had always been somewhat rumpled in the past.

And, in the fridge, there are Tupperware containers of leftovers stacked evenly. And through it all he feels as though it is he who is the guest here. As though he is intruding on another way of life, but he doesn't begrudge her that.

When Dorothy does go back to Corpus, he struggles to keep the house in order. Grocery shopping was nearly impossible because his spare time has been almost compulsively filled with checking Rita's email account and scrutinizing bank records and calling old friends. The intermittent reports from Corbett come in, tantalizing leads that direct him to one town or another, and he spends hours tracking down small-town newspapers and calling Podunk sheriff's offices hoping to gather some sort of information.

Now, as he climbs out of the pit and into the kitchen, he can hear the coffee percolating. He makes his way to the bathroom and showers and changes into clean clothes and when he returns Dorothy and Caleb are sitting at the kitchen table. There is the snick and snap of a knife on a cutting board as she cuts an apple into even eighths before slipping them into a Ziploc bag. Caleb smiles softly from his seat at the table as he inexpertly spoons Cheerios into his mouth.

"Noni's going home today."

"Just for a while, hun," she says. "Noni will be back soon."

Suddenly, it dawns on Travis that this is something that he never got from his wife, not the slightest warning that she would be leaving, nor the most cursory statement that she would – at some point – return. He glances at his son, wondering if the thought has washed over him, and hopes that it hasn't.

With the house in order, Travis helps Dorothy carry her suitcases out to the car and packs them carefully into the trunk. This has become a well-practiced routine. There in the sun washed driveway, they hug and kiss goodbye and she heaves Caleb up to hold him close, grunting with exertion. He's almost too big for her to lift anymore; this may be the last time that she will be able to lift him and hold him captive against her chest. After a moment, she lowers him slowly to the ground and he stands near her, reluctant to let her out of his sight.

"I'll be back soon," she says.

But Travis is uncertain if she is saying it to assure them or herself.

Dorothy reaches out and wraps her fingers around his arm, smiling at him with that same, knowing and apologetic look before she climbs into her car and eases out of the driveway.

Father and son watch the car shrink out of sight and disappear around the corner at the end of the block. The afternoon heat is diminishing, the sun sinking behind the tall acacia in the backyard. Travis places his hand on his son's shoulder and guides him back into the newly silent house. A silence that leaves room for Travis to harvest his memories, pressing each image between the pages of want and the unknown future. Even though he carefully preserves those thoughts and dreams, he realizes that they will eventually become brittle and dry. There will be a fragility in those memories, but at least he will have them. At least he will still be able to return to those desiccated reminders of what might have been.

There's a clear difference, he thinks as he watches Caleb arrange his cars on the living room floor, between Corbett bringing Rita back and Rita coming back on her own. Even if neither one seems any more probable than the other. The cause no longer matters because the result will be the same either way: she'll have been gone and there will be no way to return to the way that things were. Just as Corbett mentioned in their first meeting. No matter what, he will be left forever wondering when she will walk away from them again.

In the early morning, he wakes to the realization that he has dreamt of her. No. It isn't exactly Rita that he has been dreaming of, but an idealized version of her. He wonders if he had, so many years ago, fallen in love with some idealized not-her.

The Ghost of Herself

She's grown accustomed to the transience of buses and hitched rides; cut-rate motels that stink of strangers that loitered too long in their own desperation. She's become a connoisseur of motel rooms: the way the water pressure is better in one, or the way another has a softer bed. At first the rooms blurred together, and then slowly they separated out into distinct places.

And so, she appreciates that a certain room is located on the top floor where the distant freeway noise is absorbed by a too-empty parking lot. She pushes open the door and instinctively reaches down to crank the AC. The mattress sags perceptibly towards the center, and the springs give beneath her as she sits on the edge of the bed. She slips off her shoes and folds her legs beneath her as she lights a cigarette and reaches across to the nightstand where a glass ashtray sits empty save for a book of matches. As smoke catches on the updraft of air conditioning, she upends the paper Food Emporium bag on the bed. Cigarettes, hair dye, and scissors cluster on the faded bedspread and she sets to work on the cardboard and plastic packaging of the scissors. She tests the slow zip of the blades before inspecting the packet of dye with its plastic mixing tray and flimsy gloves.

How much time and energy did she invest in beauty school – how much money – only to sit in a thirty-dollar motel room with ten-dollar dye and five-dollar scissors?

Her roots have grown a quarter of an inch or more since leaving San Antonio, a physical calendar of juxtaposed salon bleached hair with nearly black roots. Her hair has become brittle from the endless desert air and hotel shampoo. Standing in front of the mirror she begins to cut haphazardly, pulling fistfuls of hair and snipping only a few inches from the roots. The physical change will now match the emotional change simmering inside her. This is a reincarnation of selves, she tells herself as clumps of hair gather in puddles at her feet like sloughed off skin.

The sun here seems to set later than she is used to. The westward sky is an empty purple as a staccato breeze cuts crossways over the parking lot, evening out the heat that has been trapped in the pavement. Standing on the walkway outside her room, the air is cool on her neck and scalp as she crosses her forearms over the still hot railing. Although she is uncertain exactly which direction to look, she knows that south, however many hundreds of miles away, a familiar house in San Antonio is growing steadily accustomed to her absence. This unfathomable distance is made up of more than just miles. It is a distance of days and weeks. It is a distance of self-doubt and isolation. Closer, she can barely hear the cars droning past like impatient flies on the nearby highway. There is the promise of ebb and flow, and the knowledge that the road that leads towards home also leads away from it.

Without having to open her wallet she knows the exact amount of cash that is still there. She is acutely aware of its dwindling. She thinks back to the true crime shows that Travis used to watch at night after Caleb went to bed. The cheesy re-enactments and overly dramatic voiceovers. There were lingering lessons there, things she had absorbed without realizing it. A job is out of the question, since it would mean providing a license or a security number, or both. Anyone looking for her would be able to track her down easily. As easily as if she had used a credit card or announced her presence on the nightly news.

At the Food Emporium, she had seen a bulletin board near the deli, one of those places where people put up fliers for free kittens and lost dogs. It had seemed a long shot, but she had stood there looking at every flier at least twice before she finally spotted the homemade flier for a maid service. Now, the dye setting in her hair, she crushes out her cigarette and walks back into the motel room, digs the small scrap of paper from her wallet and lays it beside her cigarettes. She retreats to the bathroom to watch the dye slither from her hair and down the drain.

From the phone booth in front of the motel, she dials the number on the scrap of paper. The payphone is an anachronism. Do people still use public phones like this? Coins chunk through the slot and the dial tone comes on, staticky and distant. A woman's voice answers, soft and sonorous. Rita imagines that the speaker is a maternal, middle aged woman; maybe a former teenage beauty queen. Rita introduces herself as Joanne – a name that she's been thinking about since just before she left Billy in Spokane. The name had been one that she and Travis had on their list of names before Caleb was born, and the name has lingered within her. Saying the name aloud brings to mind a fleeting image of the stranger who gave her a ride from New Mexico to Washington. The name solidifies the change even as she asks the woman if she might be looking for any extra help. And then the woman is asking Joanne if they can meet for coffee at a place only a few blocks from the motel. Joanne stands with the cold plastic of the payphone pressed to her ear as she strains against the white noise to hear the woman's directions to the diner.

Since there is little else to do but sit in her motel room and smoke, Joanne begins a slow walk to the diner, making her way down a cracked sidewalk stitched with yellow weeds and pockmarked with blackened gum. She barely looks up as she walks. She hopes this will mean a job. She can't imagine going back now. On the way, she passes a second-hand store run by the church of Saint Something-or-other. The store is full of a thick, musty smell of long abandoned closets; it's a thick smell that lingers in the aisles. She chooses a few pairs of jeans and some faded t-shirts from the men's section. In the flimsy dressing room, she sheds her old clothes and leaves them in a rumpled pile, her skin itching with the incongruity of someone else's clothes. The woman behind the counter punches numbers into an antiquated register and hands Rita her change along with the rustling bag.

"God bless, dear." The woman says.

The diner is geometrically out of sync with the low-slung strip mall and stucco apartment buildings nearby. Vaguely pentagonal, the building is sheathed in brown siding and a sloping shingled roof. Joanne takes a booth within sight of the front door, knowing that she is early as she sits there with the bag of new clothes firmly between her feet, sipping coffee.

Her stomach rumbles, but she's afraid to buy anything else in case the job falls through. The waitress drifts past, fills Joanne's coffee cup, and disappears again in a faint swishing of skirt and apron. She's on her second cup of coffee when a woman walks through the front doors and looks around the mostly empty diner. The woman is younger than Joanne expected, but even so she knows that this must be the woman that she talked to on the phone. A slim, tan woman five or six years younger than her, with long black braids flung back over her shoulders. The woman approaches cautiously and smiles.

"Joanne?"

The women shake hands and the waitress materializes, throwing the strangers into abrupt and awkward silence. The woman -- Selena was it? -- orders tea with honey, Joanne stares out the window and at the Food Emporium across the sun shimmered asphalt.

"Been here long, Joanne?"
"Fifteen minutes maybe."

"I meant here in town."

"A day or so."

"Only been here a few months myself."

The waitress returns with a small glass carafe of hot water and an empty coffee cup. Joanne smiles politely and sips her coffee, wondering what to say next. It's been a week or more since she's had a real conversation with anyone – a conversation of any substance. It seems as though days at a time have passed without her saying a word, but there is no way to be certain. It's a pendulum swing from her past life where gossip and conversation were requisite currency.

There's something about this woman, Selena, that lends itself to immediate and sincere trust, and Joanne tells herself that it must have something to do with the woman's chestnut brown eyes; even now as Selena looks at her, the prolonged eye contact nearly makes Joanne look away. It's the type of intensity that cuts all the way back to San Antonio, as if this stranger is scouring Joanne's forehead for the Mark of Cain. It's the same sincerity that Billy had and she wonders how she could be so lucky.

"I usually work alone," Selena is saying, "but truth is it isn't rocket science, Joanne. I'm guessing that you've done something like this before, cleaning houses?"

"If you count my own, then yes."

"Like I said, not rocket science. When it comes down to it, cleaning is cleaning is cleaning, and to be honest I could use the help. Don't take this wrong, Joanne, we just met, but I can't afford to work with someone who's going to try and rip off the places we're cleaning."

"I'm not the stealing type."

Here is the same x-ray gaze accompanied now by an expression that makes Joanne nervous. Is there some residual aura, maybe, something that Selena senses but can't pinpoint? It feels as though this woman is excavating deep beneath sedimentary layers of self, finding the fossilized remains of a past long since buried.

"Where are you from, Joanne?"
"San Antonio."

"You've come quite a ways. You have family around here?"

"Nope."

"If you don't mind me saying, seems like you're carrying something pretty heavy. A sadness."

"Everyone has something sad about them."

"I imagine there's more truth to that than either of us can ever really know. You're over here at the Riverside? I'm guessing that you need a job because a job is cash and I can't say that I know what you're running from, but I imagine that as long as it isn't something illegal then it really isn't any of my business, is it?"
"Unless you consider bad relationships illegal, then we should be just fine."

There's a flash of clarity and understanding in Selena's eyes – something that indicates that everything suddenly makes sense. A smile spreads across her face as she stirs her tea absently, looking at Joanne as if seeing her for the first time. For a moment, silence descends on the table again and the waitresses swish past. And then Selena leans forward, almost conspiratorially.

"Look. This may sound strange, but I have some extra room if you need a place to crash. Doesn't do you much good to make money if you're just going to turn around and spend it all on a shitty motel room."

Since she's pre-paid for the room, Joanne stays in the motel one more night, reclining on the rented bed with her feet stretched out in front of her, listening to the churn of the AC as cold air crawls down her arms. She sits, not watching TV although her eyes intermittently drift over the screen, the volume turned down to a low frequency buzz as she drifts into semi-consciousness as a new mantra loops through her mind: the past is the past is the past. She invokes the mantra to chase away memories of Travis and the image of Caleb coloring at the kitchen table, his feet swinging in sweet childhood oblivion. Rita is anchored to can't-escape-the-past, but Joanne is adrift on the swell of take-it-as-comes.

Sleep is episodic. Each time she strays back into consciousness, the light outside the room is several degrees lighter. And then it's too light to sleep and she coaxes herself from bed and looks out at the empty parking lot. It's just after five in the morning and she wonders where all the people on the highway are going; people who must be locked into careers and relationships and mortgages. People mired in student loans and medical bills. Obligated to dentist appointments and play dates. In the dimness of the room, she shovels her few belongings into her backpack. The evidence of herself that she leaves behind is becoming less and less. Here, it is only an overflowing ashtray and clumps of blond hair in a trashcan.

Just after eight, Selena pulls up outside the musty motel lobby where Joanne sits sipping acrid coffee from a Styrofoam cup. The morning air is crisp and as Joanne climbs into the passenger seat, she can see that the back of the battered four door is crowded with cleaning supplies stacked into plastic laundry baskets.

"I'd ask how you slept, but I can't imagine anyone sleeps in a place like this."
The crosstown drive is all of fifteen minutes, and Selena pulls into a trailer park tucked back behind banks of tall, narrow trees that she wishes she knew the name of. Between the

trees, Joanne can see trailers clustered like spokes around a patch of grass with picnic tables and a pathetic looking plastic play structure. The road is rumpled asphalt raised off the ground by several inches and the car jolts as Selena pulls off the asphalt and onto the square of concrete beside a boxy tan and green Winnebago.

"This is it," Selena says.

Joanne realizes – and it seems odd to her now –she has never been inside a trailer or a motor home or whatever it is that these things are called. She has passed these parks countless times, the anonymous places that line highways and crop up just outside the town limits. Maybe people would think that a woman who worked in a salon for the better part of a decade would have plenty of familiarity with trailer parks, but it had been an upper end salon that attracted more ritzy clients. The air smells of something like lavender and creosote, but inside the Winnebago it is a somehow warmer smell of tea and old paperbacks. The narrowness of the trailer leaves them standing at an awkward angle facing each other – almost unnaturally close. Selena points to a glorified shelf above the driver's seat.

"This is the guest room," she says. "I know it's not much, but it's something."

"I can't thank you enough."

"Happy to do it, Joanne. Really. You can toss your things up there. There's not much of a grand tour to be had. Bathroom is behind that folding door. My room's in the back. Sink. Fridge. Stove."

Selena's voice fades as she moves towards the back of the trailer, where Joanne can hear her opening and closing drawers. When she returns, it's with an armful of wool blankets that are usually seen around the shoulders of disaster survivors.

"We've got about a half hour before we need to get going," Selena says. "Figured that would give you some time to get settled. You hungry?" "I'm fine," Joanne says as she places a tentative foot on the driver's seat and heaves the blankets up onto the narrow shelf of a bed, reminding herself that she'll want to be careful not to sit up too quickly when she wakes in the mornings. She cautiously twists herself up into the shallow area and begins to arrange the blankets, nudging her backpack into the far corner of the space. It's the first place that she has stayed in weeks that isn't a motel room, and for the first time, she doesn't feel as though she will be leaving again in less than forty-eight hours.

There are three houses on the list to clean that morning and fortunately all of them are in the same part of town. The drive takes them through the commercial district and up a steep hill to where the sunbaked earth gives way to grass that grows greener the bigger the houses get. Selena leans over the steering wheel, peering at the address as Joanne, detached, simply stares at the palatial places that are built only a few feet from each other as though all of the money that has been spent on these monstrous homes is to occupy as much of the lot as possible, dwarfing driveways and giving the whole pre-planned neighborhood a claustrophobic feel. It seems as though the houses are built only to capture the air and lay claim to levels of territory that extend upwards from some recess beneath the ground.

"Here we go," Selena says finally, easing up to the curb within several inches of a bank of mailboxes.

They carry the mismatched laundry baskets to the door of their first house. They can hear the echo of the doorbell inside, and the soft padding of deliberate feet. The woman that answers the door is cheerful and rosy cheeked, and Joanne guesses that she must be in her mid-fifties. Considering the carefully coifed hair and French-tips of her nails, she must visit the salon at least twice a month. But the woman is

kind and affable and gives them a list of the
things that she would like to have done. Lists of
rooms and chores that make Joanne feel like a
kid again, as though her mother has just
handed her the list of things that need to
happen before she is allowed to go out and play.

Somewhere in the house, disembodied voices
of a news program float. The two women
separate and begin cleaning from opposite ends
of the house. As Joanne carts her supplies down
the hall to the guest bathroom, she passes rows
and rows of family photos and can't help but
wonder if the people that live in the house can
identify everyone in those pictures. Here are the
distant relatives and relatives of relatives
portrayed in sun faded colors, in black and
white, in sepia, in the crisp color and sharpness
of just-the-other-day.

Although she's seen her reflection in motel
mirrors and storefront windows, she had always
been able to look away. Now, here in a complete
stranger's house, she is forced to stare into her
own reflection as she cleans the bathroom
mirror in smooth even motions. Slow circles that
polish out dust and spatterings of what must be
toothpaste. Inevitably – before she can realize or
stop herself – she is thinking about the house in
San Antonio. It is a memory that lingers
indelibly against the backs of her eyelids. There
is the ghost of a scene, probably an imagined

thing, of Travis and Caleb. Every day there is another ghost – the ghost of herself – that is fading out.

The house is heavy with echoes. It isn't only the disembodied voices of TV announcers, but also the echoes of her own past, calibrated to erode her sense of separation. She slips the Windex and rags back into the basket and sets to work on the bathtub with Borax and scrubbers, scouring until her arms burn with exertion, all of the fine muscles and tendons trembling and sweat slicking the back of her neck. The smell of Borax is thick in the air now, mingling with the other chemical smells until her eyes water. When she is done scouring the bathtub, she pauses to catch her breath, the backs of her legs shaking as pins and needles assault her feet. As she stands there in the hallway, she can hear the far-off rattle of dirt and dust being sucked into the hose of a vacuum. When they are done here they will go on to another house filled with the hopes and fears and memories of people she has never met and may never see again.

A ceiling of scattered clouds diffuses the sun as they pull back into the trailer park nearly ten hours later. The smell of lavender and creosote is augmented by the smell of barbecue and the stink of the cleaning products that have absorbed into their skin.

"Never could get used to the smell," Selena says.

While Selena showers, Joanne climbs up into the bunk and rearranges the blankets around her, the wool fibers scraping against her cheek and arms. She pulls the blanket around herself and tries to shut off her brain. It's Caleb that she sees when she closes her eyes. She tries making mental lists to distract herself: places she's been since she left. A rough estimate of miles. But it's the one thing that she couldn't part with that weighs on her mind. Although the picture is within arm's reach, she no longer needs to look at it. She can call to mind all the minute details just by closing her eyes. It's late in the evening and Travis will most likely be putting him to bed by now. Perhaps reading him a bedtime story or telling him that mommy will be home soon. Travis, struggling, doing his best to comprehend what is happening and all the while trying in vain to hide the truth from their son. She knows that he will maintain optimism. He will forever jump when the phone rings thinking that she will be on the other end of the line. She wonders now if that optimism will fade. She wonders if Caleb will remember her; will there still be photos of her mingled in with

the other relatives that Caleb is unable to
identify?

The Geometry of Solitude

Route 82 cuts east-west past the front gates and save for the sound of passing semis, most days are relatively peaceful. Even so, Sandy is learning to ignore the pitch change of the massive engines describing the curvature of the hill, the whine deeper as they reach the top and then rising as they descend. An inverted function of topography.

Mid-morning sun highlights dampness on the salvia and summer snapdragon in the flower boxes surrounding the deck. It's been years since Tom made those boxes for Sandy-it was the summer she'd decided she needed a garden to occupy what she liked to think of as her dotage. This is her ideal place, whether or not anyone else might agree. As park managers, their trailer sits a stone's throw from the park entrance, and from her perch she can see the comings and goings of the residents. The location is inconvenient only when late night highlights scan across the park and engines echolocate down the narrow gravel roads. It's a side effect of the park. Here, where a handful of coddled vintage cars and overpowered motorcycles sit pristine and incongruous in front of the compass of battered Vandykes, Biltmores, Winfields, and Modulines.

People dismiss trailer parks in the same way they dismiss high-rise apartment buildings. The homes of strangers are only a backdrop, ancillary. Maybe the park itself is like the barking dog chained up behind the Jacobs'. People learn to tune out such things, passing by places that are familiar and comfortable to others. Driving cross country, behind insulating windshields and windows, strangers pass quaint houses and the broken abandoned places, not bothering to acknowledge that actual people occupy those places.

And so, she sits among her plants in the soft breeze with the familiar backdrop of mismatched trailers, reading her trashy magazine and smoking. Sometimes there are several out at a time, a surplus of glossy pages. It's precisely the level of trash that she appreciates to distract her from the world itself. She finds that they perfectly keep with her new persona as a trailer park manageress. *Manageress*, she thinks, makes her sound like Cruella Deville, a woman house-coated and slippered with gold cigarette holder. Even so, she likes it. Everyone in this magazine is no one that she cares for. These are people famous for being famous. Here, in her relative anonymity, she can flip through the pages with impunity. The Manageress presides over photo-shopped femme fatales.

Her mind drifts over the pages without registering word or image for minutes at a time, until she craves a smoke and retrieves the pack from the table. The cellophane of her cigarette pack rattles in an almost imperceptible breeze as she curves her hand around the lighter and touches flame to a fresh cigarette. A thick glass ashtray weights the pages of her magazine against the breeze.

Half an hour later, finally bored with the magazine, she lets it drop to the cedar planks at her feet. Later she will add the magazine to the growing thick stack beside the couch. Eventually, Tom will nag her to get rid of them, she'll protest but, ultimately, relent. A fire hazard, he says. Magazines are fuel tempting fate. He says: there is no reason to be stubborn. I've seen it before. Besides, he knows that she has no intention of going back to look through celebrity recipes and weight-loss secrets or fashion tips. She has neither intention nor desire to take quizzes or read articles on "How to Please Your Man" or "How to Tell If Your Lover Is Faithful."

She sits for a moment watching the wind push and pull at the flowers in her planters. She can hear Tom puttering around the other end of the trailer tinkering on one thing or another. She no longer bothers to ask what new project he's working on, and if he tells her she just as quickly forgets. There are always technical details that her mind is not built to grasp. Yet, he insists on telling her in a voice that seems to presume that she knows exactly what he is talking about. Voltage. Amperage. She takes a long last drag from her cigarette before it burns down to the orange filter and stubs out the butt not long before Tom comes around the end of the trailer and steps up onto the deck, wiping the sweat from his forehead with the edge of his faded IAFF sweatshirt.

"Have to go to the store," he says.

She nods but doesn't look up from her garden.

"Do you need anything?"

Sandy shakes her head and leans slightly into him as he puts his arm on her shoulder and kisses the top of her head. She hears him duck inside for his wallet and then he passes back down the path to where his truck is parked. The truck's deep rumble sets the dogs barking again and she can hear the gravel grind beneath the wheels and then go silent as he pulls onto the blacktop.

By the time he returns from the store she has finished with *People* and has moved on to *Us*. He makes his way back to where he was working and she hears him dropping tools – the metallic sound of one thing clanging against another. The names of the tools are familiar to her: hex wrenches and box wrenches, flatheads, Phillips. Crescent this and long handled that. Each has some elusive purpose that she'll never be able to understand. About ten or fifteen minutes later, she glances up to see Tom coming back around the trailer with a sheepish look on his face. He steps up onto the deck and lays two parts on the table – pieces that look almost identical. After a moment of rummaging through his pockets he withdraws a crumpled receipt and spreads it out on the table, smoothing it out carefully.

"I already had one," he says. "I don't know how I forgot it.

"You can take it back, though, right?"

He taps a knuckle on the receipt.

Once he has left she returns to her magazine briefly, but she's thinking back to a phone call he missed from their son several weeks ago. When she told him that John had called on his birthday, Tom had looked at her blankly for a moment, as if pausing for one of his witty retorts.

"It's not my birthday."

Still thinking that he was putting her on, she had laughed at him. When he continued with the same confused looks, she had to remind him that it wasn't his birthday but the birthday of their son.

"John?" he'd asked.

"John. Your son. John."

"Right."

For the better part of a year there have been seemingly insignificant things that have disappeared from his mind, but she had thought it was only because they were getting older. They used to tease each other about it. They used to talk about how great it would be when they were forgetful enough to buy their own Christmas presents and hide their own Easter eggs. But now there is something different, and the more that she thinks about it, the more the little details keep coming back up. All these things seem to coalesce into something that worries her more and more. At some point it had been insignificant, and so it had never bothered her. There were the forgotten doctor's appointments, and the moments that he stood in front of the coffee machine trying to remember the exact order of how to make coffee. Things that seemed only the hallmark of a dotty absent-minded retiree. But it has been a year now since the number of post-it notes around the trailer had begun to increase almost exponentially. A part of her had figured that it

was all nothing and that she was overreacting.
After all, hadn't she been guilty of forgetting
things herself on rare occasions?

After dinner, they are on the couch watching
the latest in a string of "made for TV" movies.
During a commercial break, Tom gets up and
carries their dishes into the small kitchen and
rinses them and sets them in the dishwasher.
He wipes down the table – all of this she knows
without having to turn to look. It's all one thing
after another – a routine. A habit. It's a habit
that he has built after years and years of living
in a firehouse, slowly making his way up the
ranks of the department. She thinks now of
what he was like when she first met him, all
broad shoulders and muscles and tan. They'd
joke that he liked to stand too close to the fires
he was supposed to be fighting to work on his
tan. Over time she came to understand and
know how hard he worked to become a
firefighter, beginning from the time that he was
a high school quarterback. She learned how he
spent his time playing football and struggling to
maintain good grades primarily because he
didn't want to sabotage any prospect he had of
joining the department.

Back then, Tom had been an easy, carefree,
and loquacious man spending a couple hours in
a small bar in downtown Everett where he

would drink with some of the other guys from
the department. They called him Champ
because it seemed as though there was never a
single thing that he had failed at in his entire
life. After all, forty years ago he had been the
youngest man in the department, and his easy
smile and good-natured approach to things
made him popular. He was optimistic to a fault
and endlessly determined. It helped the
comradery that the men had built up with each
other.

Over a period of weeks and months, Tom
and Sandy developed a deeper relationship; and
slowly it verged more and more on seriousness
until Tom finally proposed to her on the ferry
from downtown Seattle to Vashon Island where
they had planned to spend the evening at a
rented cabin. She can still remember every
detail of that night. She recalls the crisp breeze
that cut across the bow of the big, lumbering
hulk of a ship as he knelt down there on the
deck in the absence of other riders who had
retreated inside out of the wind. She
remembered the way that the breeze lightly
tousled his short sun-bleached hair. She
remembered the way that she had shoved her
numb hands into her pockets. Those same
hands had been numb and pale when she finally
pulled her left hand from her pocket so that he

could slip the ring onto her finger with only a happy nod.

During the early years of their marriage – and so many times throughout – she had reveled in the way that he was always such a typical guys-guy. He was the guy that, as the saying goes, all the men wanted to be and all the women wanted to sleep with. But he was hers without a doubt. His loyalty was absolute whether it was loyalty to the department or to the people he spent every day trying to save, or to his new wife. It was a loyalty that would eventually be transferred to their sons, like his unquestionable love. Both things were part of a complex calculus that divided at the same time it multiplied.

Of course, they'd still had their challenges. They'd faced the same trials and tribulations that she thinks every couple must face in a relationship that revolves around a demanding and dangerous career. The most difficult part had been the times when Tom was away, and that was always followed by the times that he was home suddenly and trying to enforce his authority. He was always and forever trying to control things at home until a single momentous argument had nearly resulted in their divorce. It was averted only through mutual tears and an agreement to work together for the greater good of the family. David and John had been so young then.

After Tom has put away the dishes and cleaned up the table, he returns to the couch and she asks him if he's heard from the guys recently from the old firehouse, though she already knows the answer. He shakes his head. A part of her thinks that he will ask her what she is talking about. What firehouse? But, of course, there are some things that maybe he could never forget. She looks at him in the pale glow of the TV as he sips his beer and notices the crow's feet and laugh lines that have etched themselves there like a map of the years that they have spent together have deepened. At some point his pale hair had once been more blond than silver, but these days those proportions have definitely reversed themselves.

She knows the intimate brail of his body: the indent of scapula, the curve of deltoid, the parenthetical scar of rotator cuff surgery. The pencil-wide scar bisecting his chest where a young doctor cut him open, spread his ribs and placed stints in his heart. He, too, must be able to read her body in the same way. Tracing the scar of the C-section she had when David was born. Lightly touching the silvery and soft stretch marks from growing too fast. The scar from the biopsy that she had during her breast cancer scare.

"You ought to call some of them," she says. "Maybe we could get together."

"Sure," he says, "some of them are still around."

"Unless they forgot about you."

"Why would they forget about me?"
"I'm teasing."

There is silence and she can tell that he has, once again, become engrossed in the show, just as she is now engrossed in memories of their youth. The show prattles on as she remembers Tom dressed in his uniform: both the dark blue daily uniform and the yellow flame-retardant suit that looked heavy and oppressive, even with its thick red suspenders crisscrossing his back. There was a certain smell to the uniform – one that she couldn't exactly place. It was a smell that was neither smoke nor fabric, and not altogether unpleasant.

After being gone for days at a time, he would return home and she would ask him how the office was. Or the boys would want to know how many people their daddy saved. It was the kind of thing boys do when they are proud of their father.

"Daddy saved a few cats from trees," he liked to say. "He helped a few old ladies cross the street."

Even though Sandy knew that Tom wasn't running into burning buildings on a daily basis, she couldn't help but worry – and that worry would strike her at odd times. It wasn't always as predictable as hearing a siren wailing in the distance. More often than not, worried thoughts seemed to push their way through her consciousness as she was standing in line at the grocery store, or picking the boys up from soccer practice. It was as if any moment that she wasn't actively occupied with some other task, her brain would drift to tragedy.

Regardless, there were plenty of things he would never tell the boys or her. Stories that would make her stomach churn. She knew, only in an abstract way, of the accidents that he had come upon and could only imagine the Hollywood-esque scenes of blood and the charred smell of burnt flesh. All of this was locked away inside him somewhere – and still was, even now as he leaned forward on the couch and heaved himself up so that he could gather another couple of beers from the refrigerator. This was pattern as well. He never bothered to ask if she wanted another beer because he knew with certainty that if he were going for another, she would also take another.

Maybe the mention of the guys from the old department was a bad idea. It's possible, isn't it, that he is avoiding them on purpose? Maybe he no longer wants to be reminded of those days and those tragedies. She knows with certainty that the lives he couldn't save weigh on him, the guilt of failure magnified and heavier than those he had been able to save. These were failures, and failure was not something that he was used to. It gnaws at him.

Just before John turned nine, Tom's department responded to a house fire. It'd been the middle of the night, and when she saw it on the news the next morning she knew it would stick with him. They'd managed to save two children and both parents, but a ten-year-old boy had been pronounced dead at the hospital. That single fire haunted him for the better part of a year. At the time, she had rationalized that it was only because John was almost the same age. But she came to understand that it wasn't the similarity to their son. It was as if there Tom used a specific algebraic scale that balanced lives saved against lives lost, and each life lost was exponentially heavier.

She had urged him, after the worst calls, to go and see someone, but he had simply shook his head. First responders didn't like to admit that they couldn't handle the trauma inflicted on them in the middle of otherwise calm afternoons. While their families were safe, across town, watching ball games they pulled devastated bodies from cars. They handed newly orphaned children stuffed animals. They stomped through the ashes of childhood homes.

"We do what has to be done," he told her. "Not an easy job."

Somewhere along the way he'd even talked John out of firefighting as a profession – not because he was worried about his son's safety – but for the pragmatism of their son actually taking advantage of the talents that he had been born with.

"It's a noble profession," Tom had told John, "but don't feel as though you have to do what I did in order to earn my respect. You're smart. Smarter than I was at your age. If you do this, do it for yourself. But you also need to know if it's what you really want to do, or if it's something that you're going to start doing and get stuck doing and wish that you had gone to college and followed a different dream."

John had taken it well and, instead of firefighting, he had attended the University of Washington's Foster School of Business. It was that same son that he had somehow forgotten – however momentarily – only six months back. She couldn't reconcile that now. She struggled to figure out why or how and tried to convince herself again that there might have been something else on his mind; perhaps he had been mulling over some project or some other idea when she'd mentioned it, and so the whole thing had been out of context and a simple mistake.

"Something bothering you?"

Sandy looks up, realizing that the show's credits are playing. Tom is leaning back in the couch looking at her at an angle, as if trying to figure out a puzzle. Self-consciously, Sandy brushes her hair back behind her ears.

"Sorry," she said. "I was just thinking.

"Lord help us when this woman starts to think. Which is it going to be for me this time? Heart-ache or wallet-ache?"

She smiles and leans towards him, resting her cheek on his shoulder, inhaling the familiar smell of aftershave, the same brand he has worn for thirty years. As she shifts towards him, he puts his arm around her and lets out a deep sigh that seems to come from the bottom of his soul.

"Who died?" he asks.

She turns to look at him, crinkling her neck.

"Who died?" he asks again. "That's what you're acting like. Like someone died."
What could she do but shake her head and assure him that everything is fine. She has had fears like this before, fears of being alone

without him, knowing that there is no way that she could ever re-marry. She could never re-love.

"Sleepy, I guess."

"Well go on to bed, just save me a place."

She debates for a moment, wondering if it would be better to stay there beside him, recalling moments that she has had with him – banking them for the day when they were gone. But she relents; she couldn't go on living as though he might die any second. There is nothing wrong with him; after all, he is still as healthy as a horse.

"Maybe I will," she says finally, and he places his hands on the small of her back to boost her up. She smiles at him sleepily and hears the couch shift and settle beneath him as she shuffles down the hall to the bedroom, her thick socks scrunching around her feet as she moves. Outside, the night is dark and she hears cars hushing out on the highway, through the slats of the blinds she sees the handful of trailers and motor homes facing them – each belonging to a family she knows by face and name. The high orange streetlamps cast down a warm familiarity on the park, and she changes by that diffused light without bothering to turn the bedside lamp on. The dog down at the Jacobs' is quiet.

She pulls back the covers and slips into the cool envelope they'd left there. She wishes only to fall into good, warm dreams; but there is no way of actually knowing what those dreams will be when she closes her eyes. A sliver of light becomes a wedge, stretching outwards from the gap beneath the door. She is trying to remember the name of that singular and specific shape: trapezoid, rhombus, parallelogram? She hears the TV murmuring in the front room despite the fact that he has adjusted the volume.

As she lies there in the darkness of their room, she wonders how long they still have with each other – as though there is some sort of time limit and at any moment a cosmic egg timer might go off and shatter the world that they have built together. And then, perhaps, the timers are reset, and it ticks only for the one that remains, the clock trickling towards their own ending. In the meantime, it would be only a purgatory of days, an endless stacking up of movie magazines with no one to remove them for her – but the plants would continue to be watered with the irrigation system that Tom had set up and the tenants would continue to bring their lot fees to her once a month. And somewhere, behind the closed doors of the other trailers, people would say how sorry they felt for her, this widow living alone in a trailer park. Or maybe, it wouldn't be her at all, perhaps it

would be Tom that stayed and she would be
gone and then there would be nothing to worry
about at all.

In Constant Return

The road has a lunar pull that eclipses all
other thoughts for days and weeks at a time.
Yet, not long after Billy returns to the road
there is a shift in gravitational pull and he
begins to think only of home. For two decades,
there has been the ebb and flow. When he is on
the road he feels pulled towards home, and
when he is home he feels pulled towards the
road. All the gravitational pull has not changed,
he's learned to relegate himself to the present
with a meditative focus his younger self would
have envied. Everything is now a carefully
articulated cycle of home and away. The only
way to sustain these trips is to become the
transitory curator of the machines he collects
and refurbishes.

Mile after mile, turn after turn, he closes in
on his house which skulks on the back corner of
the lot. Everything in his world is marked by
carefully measured increments: miles, weeks,
years, dollars, gallons of gas, and cartons of
cigarettes. The only thing that can't be
quantified is the growing ache in his knees and
the phlegmatic rattle of his cough.

He pulls into the familiar gravel driveway
and cuts the engine and studies the white
luminescence of his own house through the rain

pebbled windshield. Hazy globs of light, the reflection of the street lamps, spider-webs across the front windows. The sway of the suspension and the ticking of the cooling engine are his only company as he lights a cigarette and climbs out of the van. As he nears the front door, the motion light snaps on and he pauses like a welcomed intruder. There is the chunk of the deadbolt and then he is inside with the momentarily unfamiliar smell of vaguely musty carpet and furniture marinated in years of cigarette smoke. Soon the smell will become undetectable once again. Two bottles of whiskey and a carton of cigarettes are waiting for him in the buzzing refrigerator. In the freezer is a collection of TV dinners encased in the icy feathers of freezer burn.

It isn't until he enters the garage that he feels as though he is finally home. As the shop-lights sputter and crackle to life at the end of their chains he stands in the damp chill surveying the workshop, assuring himself that everything is as he left it. The polished concrete has the sheen of ice and each tool hangs precisely from a pegboard mounted to the wall. Arranged along the far walls, patient as sentries, stand drill press and sandblaster and band saw. The dark glass of his welding mask reflects the overhead lights from where it hangs from the oxy-acetylene rig that Shaffer gave him years ago, shortly after he had mustered out of the Navy. Satisfied by his appraisal, Billy crushes his cigarette out in the sand-filled Folgers can and sets about opening the garage door.

The rain has let up and is now roiling lightly on the hood of the van as he climbs back in and swings the old Econoline around, backing it smoothly up to the door. He will unload everything that he can on his own. Only the old Coca-Cola vending machine will have to wait until tomorrow, when he can coax Jensen over to help him lower the thing down onto the hand truck. Slowly, Billy will ease into this second-half of his life, living almost exclusively in the workshop, spending hours turning wrenches and cleaning corrosion and pitted rust from long neglected machines. Each movement is reverent, but these things are not to remain here. He is only a temporary guardian preparing them for future lives in the homes of strangers he may never meet.

It's nine in the morning and the clouds are still high and scattered, cold and distant, when Jensen arrives. Billy is in the kitchen nursing a grainy hangover, his coffee laced with Old Grandad. The two men sweat and curse as they wrestle the old machine towards the end of the van and ease it onto the hand truck. Scabs of rust have gathered on the surface of the machine and the base is dented with what might have been an impassioned kick; still the red is the unmistakable Coca-Cola red of Billy's youth. Even in its battered state, the thing exudes the magic and nostalgia of childhood. By the time he became aware of the machines they had already begun to disappear, even the one down at the drugstore. He remembers marveling at the thing that seemed bigger than his grandfather's Buick, wondering already at the secret inner workings.

Several hundred miles away and four decades in the past, Billy had schlepped the garbage out behind the apartment building. The bag skittered against the pavement with every other step. Tangled in the flotsam and jetsam beside the dumpster, Billy spotted the square base of the cast-off turntable. He knelt there beside it and cleared away the crumpled cigarette wrappers and blackened banana peels. The swing arm bent upwards and changed course midway towards the sky. He'd carried the thing surreptitiously back into the apartment, moving awkwardly up the stairs under the burden, nervous that some neighbor would chastise him for theft or for scavenging in the dumpster. Back inside the apartment, he raided the junk drawer for a screwdriver and hammer before performing an amateurish autopsy in the close quarters of his closet where his mother wouldn't see him. Through a confluence of curiosity and persistence he became steadily more proficient at taking things apart; the inner mysteries of cast off machines unraveled until he could predict the constellation of gears and motors beneath the casing of various machines.

Billy plumbed the depths of the school library for books on motors and circuits. He scoffed at the Rube Goldberg machines in his thumb worn comic books. In time, he had squirreled away enough purloined shop manuals and supplies shoplifted from the drugstore to have a sizable collection. He became adept in the use of super-glue and duct tape and in the repurposing of wire coat-hangers; his future step-father, Herb, constantly complained about the lack of hangers.

For months he slept little, toiling half-heartedly at his homework, anxious to return to his closet workshop. Despite reasonable grades, his mother never ceased nagging him about the piles of overdue technical books (many of which he could barely comprehend) and the stink of WD-40 that now permeated every room of the small apartment that they shared with Herb.

Billy had been twelve or thirteen at the time, young and beginning to resent his father's absence. Herb was a dismal replacement, sitting for hours on the couch, sweating through his threadbare t-shirts. Billy had never known his own father and knew only that the proverbial honeymoon was over before he could walk. Through the second part of middle school he fumbled alone with salvaged machines and stolen tools, his obsession growing. In the absence of salvage, he took apart the toaster and the blender, and would have made an attempt at the TV if it hadn't been under Herb's constant gaze.

And then, like a snapshot of destiny, Billy made it to high school and walked into Shaffer's third period woodworking class. That particular indoctrination was less than spectacular; his first project, a lopsided birdhouse, earned him a C so low it scraped the surface of a D, but it also earned him Shaffer's encouragement. The class was an inversion of what Billy had been teaching himself, crouched in his small closet pulling things apart. He wonders now if Shaffer could tell the frustration was a result of his constant effort to deconstruct.

At the time, Billy believed his decision to join the Navy was a byproduct of his mother's insistence that he stop dismantling perfectly good appliances. The true catalyst, he knows now, arrived clad in a stark, white uniform. Preternaturally white. As crisp as the sharp edges and creases that might have been crafted in a miter box. The recruiter had visited the shop class one fall afternoon of Billy's senior year and explained to the boys the endless opportunities available in the Navy. As the recruiter spoke, Schaffer watched with earnest respect from his seat at the front of the class. Rumors of Shaffer's exploits as a young Marine in the Korean War had instilled in them deep reverence, and their barrel-chested teacher's obvious respect for the recruiter made the prospect of military service seem the epitome of manliness.

In late April of that same year – as his classmates began to sport sweatshirts for the various colleges they would be headed off to at the end of summer – Billy stepped into the shop-room. Even after four years of taking every class Shaffer offered, it felt strange to walk into the room in the desolate silence that settled after the last bell. The room was cool and comfortable, each tool and every machine had its specific, perfect purpose and the margin of error was morbidly slim as Shaffer often reiterated as he told – with no lack of masterful skill – the purportedly true stories of the classroom disasters visited on careless students.

Even before the door clicked closed behind Billy the older man was heaving himself up from his desk. They shook hands there in the broad, empty space at the front of the classroom, Shaffer's massive paw eclipsing Billy's own, and they took seats at one of the long, graffiti tattooed tables. Billy slipped his thumbnail into the soft grooves of scratched out names and epithets that had softened at the edges over the years. Looking back, Billy could only imagine that Shaffer knew exactly why he was there. How many other students had come, just as Billy had, to seek out the advice or blessing of this surrogate father? There was that same smooth and confident silence as the two sat there, Shaffer folding his arms and waiting for Billy to begin. He didn't bother to ask Billy why he wasn't talking to his own parents. And although the words tiptoed into existence, circumspect at first, they coalesced into the sentences that Billy had turned over and over in his head hundreds of times while staring at the midnight-tinged ceiling of his bedroom. The arguments and considerations solidified there in the dry chill of the shop room.

"Sounds like you've thought this through, son."

Billy had needed neither blessing nor advice. He needed only to articulate the reason he was making the decision to someone who would neither judge nor question. The older man seemed to fill the echoing space with a neutral presence that allowed Billy to construct his certainty.

Several weeks after graduation, Billy boarded a bus for Naval Station Great Lakes. Things were uncertain then, in 1974, with the Vietnam War winding down and whispers of Cold War enmity hung like a goiter at the throat of the nation. Although there were a handful of people there to see the bus off, it was nothing like what he imagined. Shaffer didn't show up and his mother didn't cry. Herb stood beside her, impatiently shifting his weight from foot to foot. As far as Billy could tell, no one else on the bus was headed to basic training. He hugged his mother, certain she must be thinking she was losing him; his father had left first, and now he was leaving, and all that was left was the rent-controlled apartment and Herb's crumpled T-shirts sitting at the foot of the bed.

The only thing that interrupts Billy's week-long hermitage are his Saturday treks into town. By planning a little further ahead, he could just as easily limit his trips to once a month, but, as always, there is something small that he needs from the hardware store that forces him to head into town early: a specific grit of sandpaper, the right size-locking nut, more sheet-metal screws. And then there is the

relative comfort of Shirley's Diner on Dayton.
The diner, like the hardware store, has been
there so long that they seem to predate the town
itself. Both places have changed hands and
names so many times that it's almost laughable.
But names are only surface things. What
matters is that the soul of these places remain
constant. The yellow hue of the walls grows
deeper every year, stained with cigarette smoke
and atomized grease. The booths are scratched
and mended with Frankensteinian sutures of
duct tape and hot glue. The walls are tiled with
faded photos of famous and semi-famous
patrons, tiled with generations of Little League
teams the restaurant has sponsored.

Billy perches at the counter, stubbornly
refusing to admit to himself that he is here to
see Dianne. He is here to get a decent meal,
although he would readily admit that the word
"decent" barely applies. The hash browns come
in large frozen bags, burnt coffee percolates for
the better part of the day, and the pancake mix
comes in ten-pound bags of snowy powder. But
he knows, with unadmitted certainty, that
Dianne's usual shift is Saturday morning and
that she will be, more often than not, his
waitress if and when he pulls up a seat at the
counter.

Among other things, Billy refuses to admit
to himself that he still remembers a long

weekend at the coast in a rented cabin with an intermittently leaking roof and eaves that caught the high wail of the ocean squalls like banshees singing in octaves. Over time, he has felt more and more guilt for leaving her for the road. For years he thought that there would be time; which is why he resented her assertion that he was running away from reality, hiding in the open spaces of the road, and loitering in a lack of commitment that bordered on juvenile.

Billy takes a seat in the middle of the abandoned counter, the cracked Formica punctuated with dingy metal boxes of napkins and coffee cups turned upside down on white paper doilies. He instinctively turns the cup over as he sits and sets his car keys and cigarettes on the counter. Long gone are the days that smoking was allowed inside, but old habits die hard. Jensen's narrow back is visible through the long, rectangular window into the kitchen; a fringe of black hair encircles his bald, sweat-glistened pate. Dianne is several tables down talking to a handful of local boys. He knows from the camber of her hip and the half smirk that she's giving as good as she's getting.

"Well mister," Dianne promenades behind the counter, "about time you made your weekly appearance."

"Just got back day before yesterday."

"Jensen said he was over at your place the other day."

Dianne pours coffee from the carafe veritably welded to her hand, setting it down only to scribble Billy's order on her small pad of paper, not bothering to ask what he wants; his order hasn't changed in the better part of a decade, and writing it down is only a familiarity so that Jensen knows he's here. Dianne will pause and chat with him intermittently as he eats his breakfast. Perennially runny eggs on perennially burnt toast.

Dianne seems to have grown reedier; her hips are somehow wider. There is a shock of gray and brown at the front of her hair now, standing out against the raven black that she's been dying twice a month since before they met. He's seen her do this, standing at the bathroom sink in a pair of boxer shorts and a dye spattered *Rush* T-shirt. He'd stood in the doorway as she smeared Vaseline along her hairline to avoid dying her skin. He watched as the dye slowly covered the mousy brown of her roots. He runs a thumb along his lower lip as he considers the inevitability of change. Not only hers, but his. But his change has been of an unconscious sort. The road hasn't always been kind to him, constant sun and odd hours deepening his wrinkles, but if it weren't for the hours that he spends in the garage hoisting machines and twisting wrenches, he would have surely gained another ten pounds by now.

Out of the corner of his eye, he can see the ice machine in the kitchen. It's been about a decade since Jensen asked him to come by and take a closer look at the battered appliance. It wasn't that Billy had some sort of expertise with industrial kitchen appliances, but rather that he could lend his mechanical inclination to the machine and hopefully coax it back to life. It was there that he really got to know Dianne, who hadn't given up smoking yet. The two of them stood out in front of the diner with their cigarettes – she was just finishing her shift when he had finally resurrected the old machine. It wasn't long before they were dating. Or at least, some semblance of dating, as he was often leaving. She had two daughters who were grown and off starting their own lives, one already with a daughter of her own and the other is at the state college. He was an anomaly, she told him; it was odd that he should be unattached, but over time it began to make sense to her. There was a way he had of distancing himself from everything around him, like a bottle floating in the ocean, she said, unmoored and restless. After that conversation, he had refurbished an old jukebox and tried to give it to her but she had refused, knowing that

it was something that he could make a good deal
of money on.

Dianne drops his check in front of him, the
carefully creased piece of paper with her
hieroglyphic scrawl. He digs into his pocket and
unwraps the brittle rubber bands from his
wallet, plucking out a twenty and dropping it on
the counter as he draws a cigarette from his
pack and sticks it perfunctorily in the corner of
his mouth.

"There you go slinking off again," she says
behind him, but he simply turns and nods
towards her.

"See you next weekend," he says.

"It's a date," she winks conspiratorially.

At home again, Billy begins to disassemble
the Vendo 83, removing the motor and laying it
aside, taking pictures at regular intervals so
that he can move backwards through the
process when necessary. His world now is made
up of voltage readers and socket wrenches and
grease that highlights the cracks and wrinkles
of his hands, grime seeping beneath his
fingernails. Late into the night, he stands in
front of the sandblaster clearing that vibrant
red from the outer surfaces of the machine.
Neck aching as he peers through the broad
tempered glass, he watches the dark gray of raw

metal reveal itself. Billy works intermittently on other projects, rewiring old appliances and power tools with rote distraction until his thoughts are hijacked by the Vendo: the coin operation system, the refrigerator coils, the insulation he will mold into the pocket of the door.

Billy enters the house for the express reasons of eating or sleeping or shitting. He eats his TV dinners standing up at the kitchen counter, leaning against the sink, the thin cellophane sticking to the underside of the tray where he hasn't bothered to peel it back completely. In the living room, the ashtray is overflowing and the beer cans are stacked in an ever-growing pyramid.

It's strange, he thinks as he makes his was down the hallway into the kitchen, how easily two people can fall back into a rhythm, even if that rhythm has been on pause for the better part of a decade. It's well after midnight and the moon casts hazy shadows on the floor as he turns on the kitchen light and cracks open a beer. The dinner dishes are still sitting there beside the sink, and he smiles as he thinks of the woman that is, at this very moment, asleep in his bed. He is no longer worried about being caught there by the woman who has, once again, become his lover. He stands in the middle of the kitchen, unabashed in threadbare boxers, cold linoleum beneath his feet. He no longer has the lean muscle that he had when he was in the Navy, and the hacking cough of a long-time smoker is often trailed by a growling phlegmatic rattle. Yet it seems she either hasn't noticed or doesn't care.

He's been back for a month, give or take a day or two, and still the old vending machine is nestled in the corner of the garage where he left it. The men had razzed him for it, accusing him of adhering to nostalgic kitsch.

"You ought to work on cars," Dawes had said. "It'd be a hell of a lot easier."

"At least they come with wheels," Jensen added.

Cars hold only a distant attraction for him because it's always been about the way that these machines work – the way that different projects presented new and dynamic challenges. The pinball machine, for example, that he brought back from the same trip has already been fixed up and sold off, a project completed solely for the money. The internal workings of the thing, so far as he was concerned, were less artistry than functionality. The vending machine, though, required a different skill set completely. A confluence of ingenuity and adoration. There were pieces that had to be fitted just right in order for the machine to work. There was a temperamental nature that, perhaps, he could get with a car, but then it would take him much longer. In truth, he feared that he wouldn't be able to part with something that he had labored over for months at a time. Besides, the way that the machine had survived was a testament to the way that people had seen it every day, the people had plunked coins through the slot in anticipation of a reward.

A draft cuts across the kitchen as he stares at the dishes in the sink, wondering if this is how people slip down the precipitous slope into comfort and marriage. Marriage had always seemed like something of a surrender or sublimation of self. He finishes his beer and crushes out the cigarette he lit while thinking about the machine. He turns the kitchen light off and stands there in the semi-darkness, swathed in the chill of the house. The draft against his naked skin, goose pimpling his arms and back. He lets the cold build; lets the soft breath of late night and early morning linger on his skin – sinking into his pores, knowing that when he returns to the bedroom and slips beneath the sheets there will be the overwhelming comfort of warmth, like a hot shower on a winter day.

As he slips back into bed, Dianne rolls towards him without waking, the rhythm of her breathing static. He can just make out the soft creases of her face in the dimness. He barely remembers what her body had been like a decade ago in the same way that she can probably barely remember the way his felt. The skin smoother. The hair more dark than gray. But these things would have changed no matter what and there is no way to recapture that past. He doubts that he would want to, even if it was within his realm of possibility. After all, is there any reason to go about living in the past wishing that things had been different? Weren't they all simply machines that were becoming more and more antique by the day?

In the familiarity of his bedroom, in the house that has been his and his alone for years at a time; her breath tickles the fine hairs on his shoulder. And he thinks now of the reason that they had broken up in the first place. It had been primarily because he had refused to surrender himself to her and wonders for the first time if that had been a mistake. Maybe he is beginning to give into the idea of letting himself simply be with one person for the rest of his life. Maybe life has a way of wearing people down. For so long, he has refused to stay in town and adopt the mundane existence of his neighbors. It's an existence that he can barely imagine, even at the fringes of full consciousness, which he is drifting slowly away from. Everyone here, Dianne included, seems to have some sort of world that they are always, inevitably and arduously, working to maintain. The mundane – even at its most exciting – becomes dull, losing its varnish. Cracking. Pock marks of rust appearing on the surface. He's felt it hundreds of times as he cruised the backroads of America looking for the things that other people had long since cast off as useless, or broken, or outdated. But he is all of these things as well, and perhaps, the curator might soon find himself among the curated.

Torn Photographs

It had been a long three years for Rita. Years cut short by the abrupt collapse of their relationship, like a decaying empire that tumbled suddenly into ruin. Although they had never talked about it, she assumed she would marry Alan someday and they would live happily ever after. But the end of the relationship was sudden and immediate and irrevocable. One night after leaving a holiday party, they stood outside of her apartment in Corpus Christi and Alan said that they "couldn't go on like this."

For a moment she wasn't sure exactly what he was talking about. It wasn't until she turned to look at him that she noticed he couldn't look at her. There had been fights, sure. Some of those fights had been real knock-down, drag-out affairs that left them both reeling as if a gale force of anger had decimated them. But things had been going well lately; they hadn't argued at the party. Maybe it was like they said about people who chose to commit suicide – that oftentimes they did it when things were going well – before things could get painful again. The "space between them," he said, was "too distant to be closed."

Standing on the curb in front of her studio apartment in the dull orange of the streetlamps, she became aware of other people laughing and talking, passing up and down the street. These carefree strangers were oblivious to what was happening. A sense of futility had dawned on her. There was no way to make reparations now; an investment of three years disintegrated before her eyes. She didn't bother to watch him walk away; instead she turned, unlocked the door, and slammed it closed behind her.

Less than a month later, she was moving out of her apartment and heading for San Antonio, where an old high school friend happened to know of a salon that would be hiring. She was only a few years out of beauty school then, but she was confident and capable and the salon had hired her almost on the spot when she drove up for the interview shortly after the New Year. San Antonio was a chance to reclaim her forgotten self.

The joke among stylists was new man, new hair style, and true to form, Rita decided for something different now that she was at least three hours from home and living in an apartment with two of the other stylists. It was late one night after the salon was closed that the other girls set to work cutting and trimming and dying until Rita's once carefully layered hair was a slick 1940s bob with a straight fringe of bangs. They dyed her hair a deep auburn that was bright in the sun and sultry in the dark.

She fell into the new rhythm easily, letting months pass as she got used to the new city, slowly accumulating new clients. It matched her, she felt, the new city and the new haircut and the new friends. She had all but severed her ties with the people that she had known while she was dating Alan. There were too many shared memories there for her to exist in a space that she had shared with someone else for so long. And besides, the new friends knew only her. She was no longer part of a pair. No longer trying to suss out if she was hero or side kick. Barely twenty-four, she had started dating Alan just shy of her twenty-first birthday, and it was a new experience to be able to go out with the girls and enjoy herself in the bars along the River Walk. The three of them would take their time getting ready and then head out to the bars to flirt and dance and drink. It seemed cliché, but she was having fun and getting to know who she was for the first time. She knew that back in Corpus her mother would frown at her short skirts and thick eye make-up, but she didn't care. She teased the men who reminded her too much of her father – never giving them a chance - and reveling in getting some reaction from the otherwise stoic Texan boys.

And so, things went on like this for months. Spring cruised through summer, summer cruised back into fall, and as the weather was beginning to cool, one of the regular clients asked if she would like to come to a Halloween party. Although she had demurred at first, she had eventually relented. There was, as far as she could tell, no real reason not to go, and the roommates would no doubt join her. She quickly discovered that this particular Halloween party was a well-known annual tradition. They'd sipped gin and tonics as they transformed themselves into sexy gangsters in pinstripe pencil skirts, toting plastic Tommy-guns. By the time they made it to the party, they were sipping whisky from requisite flasks.

It was impossible to remember exactly when she started talking to Travis, dressed in an almost too-elaborate Revolutionary War costume, which she later learned was his default costume, a side-effect of teaching American History at Kennedy High. She'd found herself standing next to him at some point and mistaking him for a pirate.

"Where's your sword, matey?"
"Close in time period, off on terrain."

"Sorry?"
"This, I'll have you know, is a nearly accurate Colonial Rebel Replica."

This amused her. There was something about the self-effacing pride that he took in his costume; proud of himself for being just geeky enough to pull it off, and just brave enough to carry off the knee socks and buckled shoes.

"I guess we're both living out our fantasy as rebels, then?"

"Who said it's a fantasy?" She said, aiming the Tommy gun at him.

"Fair enough, muskets are no match for Tommy guns."

And, somehow, they ended up spending the better part of the evening talking – even dancing once. She had persisted enough to drag him out for two or three songs where he danced self-consciously, his hat periodically falling down over his eyes or tumbling to the ground. Finally, they'd stepped outside so she could smoke and he stood there with her, perched on the porch railing, watching her light cigarette after cigarette.

Travis was an anomaly to her, a California kid who grew up in LA prep schools jockeying with his two older brothers for the attention of their architect father and paralegal mother. And then he'd gone off to college at Berkeley and found a job out here in Texas as a teacher. She had a hard time wrapping her head around the decision to move from what seemed like such an

idyllic place as California but they were both
transplants now, people wholly unfamiliar with
San Antonio's ins and outs.

He was the first man that she could
remember – since high school – asking her out
on an actual date. And the dates themselves
were sweet and tender. Dinner at nice
restaurants and plays that nearly bored her to
tears. Yet she reveled in pushing Travis outside
of his comfort zone. Reveled in getting him to go
skinny dipping for the first time while on a trip
back down to Corpus Christi. He was smart, but
predictable and safe. He was a romantic – if not
spontaneous, then at least in a pre-planned
fashion that showed her that he had put time
and thought into his plans. And so, things began
to develop, and she began to think that he was
the type of man she deserved.

After a year they moved in together. They
rented a two-bedroom house near the
interchange of Highways' 358 and 286. It was
small but it was theirs, even if they could barely
afford it. Her father had a hard enough time
believing that his twenty-five-year-old daughter
had kissed a man, let alone slept with one. Now
they were living together, unwed. But he had
been won over by Travis's intelligence and self-

efficacy and self-deprecation. Although they saw him as a foreigner – someone from some place that wasn't quite their own territory, they began to accept him. Soon they were travelling to Corpus every few months to visit her parents, even if it meant that Travis would be relegated to the couch and she would have to sneak out in the middle of the night to make love to him. The taboo of making love on her parents' couch while they were asleep in the next room aroused in her something giddy and daring; but she also fed on the idea that he was tormented with embarrassment and anticipation of capture.

After another year they were married and had bought a house in a preplanned suburb of San Antonio, not far from Kennedy High where he was still working, and across town from the salon where she had been working for years. For several months boxes lined the walls of the living room and drop clothes spread across the living room floor. It was one afternoon, while Travis rollered white paint onto the walls, that she sat in the still unfamiliar bathroom staring at the pregnancy test. It was impossible to tell if she felt hope or dread.

When she told him that evening when he got home from work he was excited, but checked his excitement to question hers. Even then, several hours after discovering she was pregnant, she had no way of knowing or deciding exactly how she felt about the entire situation. Suddenly she had catapulted forward into adulthood: married and paying off a mortgage with a child on the way. It felt as though her own life had once again been usurped by the wants and needs of someone else. She hadn't even realized it was happening. She acquiesced to all of it because she wanted it, but she wanted it mostly because she knew that it made Travis happy. Now she wondered when and how she had sublimated herself.

The birth was everything that she had anticipated and everything that she never could have. Hours of labor and finally the nurse was laying their son on Rita's chest and she was looking at the scrunched face and slightly conical head and thinking that this was what makes it all worth it – not just the labor, but the marriage and the sublimation and the loss of self.

When Caleb was several years older, they took him down to Corpus for his birthday to visit Noni and Papa and spent a long sundrenched weekend by the beach. As they splashed and played in the water, Travis stood with his son, the two of them facing the waves,

the rhythmic in and out chasing both of them
back several feet. Caleb squealed in delight,
reminding her of everything that she loves
about this. Everything that she loves about
motherhood. Everything that she loves about
becoming spontaneous again with their young
son. The sudden trips to the zoo or down to the
ice-cream shop. She cherishes the waffle dinners
that she makes when Travis has parent night
and comes home late, wondering why for all the
world she made waffles for dinner.

She stood back a ways, watching them while
talking light-heartedly to her sister. Her sister's
own kids, sullen teenagers at the time, skulked
by the car, refusing to come out into the wind.
Rita wondered what brought them to this state
so that they could no longer enjoy the world for
what it was. Rita's sister, Stacy, had a camera
and she called Travis's name. When he turned
and saw the camera, he scooped up his giggling
son and held him in front of the perfect
spontaneity of the ocean and Stacy snapped the
picture. When the picture arrived by mail
several weeks later, framed with a thoughtful
note from Stacy, Rita placed it carefully on the
bedside table so that she could wake up to the
image. So that she could wake up to the moment
that was then.

It's not long after Caleb's fourth birthday that Rita discovered she was pregnant again. Neither of them had planned it. She suspected it happened because she had been careless when taking her birth control, missing a day here and there. Though, there was a shadow of an admission that maybe it was intentional.

Sitting in the same small bathroom staring at a nearly identical pregnancy test she had taken years before, she felt far more elated than she had upon discovering she was pregnant the first time. She thought about how nice it would be if they had a little girl. Someone that would take after her. Although, knowing the way that these things work, the second child would take after Travis, but at least there would be a yin and yang to their family. Father and daughter would be able to bond over their love of planning things meticulously. She and Caleb would disappear for adventures. She would know which child she should surprise at school — sometime just after lunch, and whisk him off to somewhere else. She dreamt of doing all the things that she wished her own mother had done.

This child will draw her even closer to Travis, cementing them as a family and giving Caleb a playmate. Perhaps Caleb will be selfish at first, but what young child wouldn't be jealous of a newborn baby, the attention divided suddenly and uneven between them. But they would get by. Things would smooth out and they would be a happy family.

When Rita first saw the blood, she dismissed it. After all, doctors had said that some bleeding during pregnancy was normal. But the blood quickly changed tempo and became a faucet, opening up. Curled into a ball on their bed, towels pressed between her legs, she called Travis in the middle of class and pleaded for him to come home. He hesitated, but only until he heard the concern and fear in her voice. She knows because she was afraid of the sound of her own voice. She was afraid of what weakness she was betraying, even to him, the one she loves so much. She thought about Caleb who was at day care and wonders what to do.

As soon as Travis pulled into the driveway, tires screeching, Rita walked out to the car and well on their way to the hospital when she panics, realizing she doesn't know where Caleb is.

"He's with Thomas," Travis said, white-knuckled. To his credit, he handled the emergency with calm. This was not something that he could have or would have planned for, and she could tell that his teeth were on edge, but he kept an even keel, driving, if anything, far too slow. Slow enough that she wanted to bellow at him. She wanted to yell at the top of her lungs that something was wrong. Something was wrong. Something was wrong.

The nurses were efficient. They asked her specific questions without betraying their own suspicions or concerns. And then she was sent down for an ultrasound, the technician parring Travis's questions by saying that she could only take the picture and it was up to the doctor to decipher them. Even at such a stressful time, he was unable to be confrontational and stopped arguing. She wanted him to demand to know. She wanted him to insist that they tell him everything that was going on. Part of her wanted him to get volatile, to show an intensity of emotion. Just for once. To take charge. To be aggressive. But it was too late.

And then the Ob-Gyn and the nurse were crouched before her, performing some procedure with machines that she couldn't identify. And then it was clear, although it needn't be said, that the baby was gone.

In the wake of the miscarriage, Dorothy and Stan came up several times to visit, staying at a nearby hotel so as not to crowd them. While Rita took time off work, Dorothy happily went about the housework, cooking and cleaning and shopping. And yet Travis felt crowded out by his in-laws. He felt as though his mother in-law had begun to make the decisions around the house — overtaking the role of his wife who seemed all too willing to surrender the responsibility.

In search of refuge, Travis retreated to the garage where he fumbled for some excuse to occupy himself. It hadn't taken long for Stan to come out to investigate, and almost immediately it was as if Travis were only visiting. The dominion of tools and fishing gear and the stink of oil and grease seemed to belong to the older man. Travis was acutely aware that he lacked the knowledge of these quintessentially masculine things. He had only the knowledge of history and literature. The knowledge of the liberal ideals that were so derided by his in-laws. Suddenly it seemed that whenever he entered his own house, it was to conservative talk shows and high calorie dinners and his father-in-law's spit cup as he sat with a chaw of tobacco tucked under his lip.

When the in-laws went home, the emptiness they left behind seemed like an abandoned dream. Their thoughts of the perfect family unit were shattered. Rita and Travis both wondered – albeit independently—if the momentary presence of her parents had magnified their suffering. Perhaps it would have been better for them to have grieved and make sense of things on their own. Instead a wall rose between them, cutting their lines of communication to each other. There had been no room to speak there in the house with other people. There had been the need but never the opportunity. When they did try to make sense of it, they lost momentum and allowed themselves to drift away from the subject. There was no need to talk about it after all that time. Travis hesitated to bring up the topic because he did not want to hurt Rita. He felt as though the simple act of mentioning the miscarriage might catapult her back into depression and anxiety. There was no need to make things worse because the suffering was there beneath the surface every time he looked at her.

Rita would not bring it up because there was nothing that she felt needed bringing up. She thought about that day often – the entire event from pregnancy test to the drive home from the hospital. It seemed as though the entire thing was done and there was nothing left to talk about. The miscarriage had the ultimate word of finality of the situation, and, at the very least, they had each other and they had Caleb. And so, selfishly, she would not say anything about it unless Travis brought it up, if Travis needed to make sense of it. The whole thing made no sense to her, but she could accept that. It was Travis who would forever struggle with the sheer abstractness of the event.

One summer afternoon, Rita dragged the plastic kiddy pool from the garage and sat it in the middle of the yard. She turned on the garden hose, and let the water slush into the small pool, pummeling the thin plastic walls with staccato rhythm. She stood there in her shorts and her broad, straw cowboy hat thinking about the emptiness of the house, like the emptiness of her womb. A thing that could be occupied – but for now was empty. Eventually, this house along with all other houses will be torn down, or burnt down, or forgotten. The places that were once special will decay. Or the memories that were made in one house will be obliterated as soon as a family moves. A house is only a shell, after all; a husk, a cocoon.

People become so infatuated with the outward appearance of a house, but for her it would be only too easy to forget weeding and mowing and watering. It would be easy to forget about hanging Christmas lights from the gutter and placing jack-o-lanterns on the front porch. And just as easy to forget to take those lights down, or throw the jack-o-lantern out. All of that was for other people. And now she realized that for years, most of what she had done was help women change themselves for others. Women who changed their hair for husbands and boyfriends. Women who changed their hair for new jobs. Women who had their hair styled for proms and weddings and first dates and job interviews and big meetings. It all seemed a paltry thing now. A facet of this particular world that she was realizing she could not completely comprehend.

But there were those who changed for themselves. There were those who altered things to change their prospective – to change their reality or shift their reality. And maybe that's what drew her to it in the first place – this prospect of rebirth and rejuvenation. This prospect of reinventing the self, working with some strange alchemy of personality and reality. It was like a mask or a disguise or a split personality.

She can feel this change bubbling beneath the surface. A desire to change, or for change, although she wasn't exactly sure which. A desire for spontaneity. She thinks back to the first time that she cut her own hair – a distant past that seemed to belong to someone else. It had been in middle school, seventh or eighth grade, maybe. Rita had come home from school after a particularly rough day and locked herself in the bathroom and cut jagged edges into her hair, cutting at a precipitous angle until the even edge of her hair was choppy and chaotic. Using Hydrogen Peroxide that had been tucked back in the medicine cabinet, she worked the clear liquid through strands of hair in the front, hoping this would make her look tough and maybe even a little dangerous. Dots of peroxide dappled her favorite dark T-shirt, like white and yellow spittle. And when she finally opened her door her mother took one look at Rita as if the world had ended.

"What have you done?"

And then she had been taken straight to the salon – her mother's favorite place to be other than the kitchen or the garden – and the stylist had set to work evening things out. It turned into a compromise, facilitated by this new co-conspirator, the stylist who winked slyly to Rita in the mirror when Dorothy wasn't looking. She had realized the power of change. The power of quiet subversion.

How many times had Rita made the trip? Her tires alone might have worn the road into pale grooves. The endless shuttling from house to school to house or grocery store to home and then back to school, or maybe day care, depending on whether or not she needed to work or needed to get things done. This was the rhythm that fell on her. At the end of the day she would return home with Caleb and make dinner and wait for Travis to come home, exhausted, with stories of frustration or occasional elation. Their conversations no longer wandered even abstractly towards travel or adventure. Everything was couched in the words of "one day." One day they would plan a vacation. One day they would visit another country. One day they would drop everything and change. One day.

But the farthest Rita had ever travelled was just beyond the state line into Arkansas to visit some distant relations, and a week-long honeymoon to Puerto Vallarta. There hadn't been a great amount of sightseeing on either trip. For the most part, the honeymoon was filled with carefully planned outings and adventures: parasailing and snorkeling and wandering the markets. But now she was beginning to suspect that even if there was a vacation somewhere in their future, the excitement of it would be sapped by the planning and re-planning.

Rita wasn't exactly sure where in the course of the drive to the elementary school that she began to think of it. Somewhere, it simply became the best option. But first she will drop Caleb safely at school and she will say goodbye to him. She will have to get that far before she can make up her mind with any degree of certainty. She needed to feel what it might be like to say goodbye to him for the last time. Or, at least to say goodbye to him without any certainty of when she might see him again. And then she will climb back in the car and she will drive home and she will pack. She will pack her things and take the picture from the bedside table, and then if she was still convinced, she will drive to the bank and then down the street to the Greyhound Station.

At the school, she left the car and walked with Caleb to the small outside area where the kindergartners line up in the morning. The sky was high and empty and nearly white with its pale blue; it's already warm outside but the breeze was cool and felt comfortable to her. The teachers were smiling and Caleb began pulling away from her towards where his friends were waiting.

"Hold on a sec, give mommy a hug goodbye."

"Why?"

"Because that's what we do when we say goodbye."

"Not always."

"Well, starting now," she said, trying not to hold him for too long. Trying to keep her emotions in check because she knows if she focused only on the feeling of leaving him behind that she will never leave. And then he was pulling away again, shouting goodbye over his shoulder and running towards his friends.

She doesn't cry until she reached the house
and was safely inside. After a few moments of
tossing her clothes onto the bed, she took a
break and collapsed on top of them. Maybe this
was all that she needed. Maybe she only needed
this feeling to remember how much she
appreciated her son and how much she
appreciated her husband and their house. After
all, her goodbye to Travis that morning had
been as cursory as it usually had.

But then, maybe that was simply a
symptom of something much greater. Even if
she were to stay, then things would simply
revert back to that same status quo at some
point. There would be no way to escape it.
Everything would go on at its sickeningly idyllic
clip. And then in five or ten or twenty years she
will realize that maybe she should have left.
Caleb would hate her for leaving, but, in a way,
it would be for him. He would know that things
sometimes disappear from our lives, and that
nothing was predictable. He will know then to
appreciate what he has while he has it. And
Travis will survive. He will be better off without
her. He will find someone else who loves him
more deeply and loves him more immediately.
Someone who will appreciate everything that he
does on an everyday basis. Lastly, she will be
doing it for herself. She will be doing it to free

herself and realize who she really was and what she wants from the world.

She heaved herself up off of the bed, her throat tight and aching from crying and the sheets and clothes rumpled from where she had twisted herself up in them. She needed to move more quickly because it was almost nine, and she wanted to be gone well before the daycare called Travis at the school to tell him that she hadn't been by yet. She will want to be somewhere where there was no turning back, so that there was no chance that she will be interrupted or called back. She will simply have to escape the gravitational pull of the city, then the state, and she will be free.

She finished packing and then picked up the framed picture of Travis and Caleb on the beach down in Corpus. She will take this with her. She will look at the picture and she will remember why it was that she had left in the first place — not out of hate for them, but out of love. Out of a desire to make their lives better. On a scrap of paper she wrote only the word "Sorry" and tucked it into the frame. She stared at the small scrap of paper for the better part of ten minutes, trying to find something more worth saying, but there was nothing else to say.

And then she was out the door and into the car and already driving across town towards the bank. She made it through the first part, and part of her actually felt better as she moved. She felt as though she was making the right decision. Everything was flowing towards the way that things ought to be and some sort of restoration of universal balance of karmic energy. Or, perhaps she was being guided by angels or by devils. All that she knew was that she doesn't care for the reason, only that there was an absolute bliss in what she was doing.

The teller behind the counter doesn't flinch or really bat an eye when Rita tells him that she would like to take out three thousand dollars from her bank account. The man behind the counter simply takes her ID and bank card and processes the request, counting out twenty-dollar bills, locking and unlocking the drawer beside his station and disappearing only for a moment to get the rest of her funds, which he placed into a neat bank envelope. The envelope was thick, but she knows that the money will go quickly, and she only hopes that she will find some sort of solution before it runs out.

She drove down the street to the Greyhound station and parked in the lot. She paused only a moment before reconsidering and moved the car into the long-term parking lot towards the back where it will be less visible and no one would think to bother it. She took on the air of a fugitive or a spy and she was thinking only of her escape. She pushed aside all thoughts of

Caleb and Travis. She knew that if she thought of them, she would be drawn back. She tells herself twice that she will return: once as she entered the building and once as she stepped up to the kiosk to buy her ticket. She can always come back. But a second part of her believed that she would not come back, that she had absolutely no intention of doing so. As soon as she leaves, she will be gone.

Ticket in hand, money stuffed into her front pocket, she sat in one of the plastic seats to wait for the bus. She bought a ticket for the next place outside of Texas. Albuquerque seemed like a logical place. While she sat, she watched the busses load and unload and the other passengers who milled about in the waiting area. She was tempted to buy a cup of coffee but thought it better to lie low. The fewer people that she interacted with, the better.

She took a deep breath as she boarded the bus, as if about to dive under frigid water. They slowly passed through town and made their way through late afternoon traffic. The digital reader-board on the side of an insurance company read just after two in the afternoon. Within the hour, Travis will get a call from the daycare letting him know that she had not picked up Caleb. And then she will have another hour or so before the two of them actually get back to the house. A two-hour head start, perhaps even longer if he thought that she was working or that she had gone down to Corpus for the weekend.

She was fitful on the ride. Wondering at the miles. Wishing that she hadn't tossed her cell phone into the dumpster outside the Greyhound station and wishing that she could call Travis to tell him that she was okay. Her mind had shifted from being excited to anxious to guilty. All she could do was close her eyes and hope to drift into a different dream. At some point, the bus pulled into a station only an hour or two from Albuquerque. She had been on the bus through the night, awake each time it had made a stop at one station or another to load or unload or to change drivers. Those stops seemed interminable. And then she was awake and wondering again what a spy would do. She grabbed her bag and got off the bus to make her way into the station. Just up the street she saw a sign for a diner, almost out of view. She walked towards it like a beacon. The early morning air cutting frigidly through her sweatshirt. Chill of the desert night. Inside, the diner was empty and she wondered then if she would be forever stranded.

Catching Up

Years after she left San Antonio – leaving behind her husband and her five-year-old son – Joanne is sitting in the small café where she works. Her hair is long now, its natural color no longer obscured by dyes and bleaches. It's been the better part of several years since she even wore makeup, and she sits there in the small café, listening to the growl of the espresso machine and the clatter of plates and the conversations of complete strangers at the next table. All of this has become white noise. The drone of daily activity is broken, but it takes her a moment to realize why. At a table not far away, a mother is talking to her five-year-old son; she's called him Caleb. Although Joanne has heard the name a number of time over the years, she's caught by the visual and auditory confluence as she realizes that she has been watching the boy for several minutes, even before his mother said his name. The resemblance is uncanny. The boy is tow headed and well behaved. As he sits there, he notices Joanne staring at him.

"Mommy, why is that lady looking at me?"

The woman glances over at Joanne and Joanne smiles and looks shyly away.

"Because you're such a handsome boy," the mother says, reaching out to smooth the boy's hair down where it has begun to stick up in the back. But the hair is stubborn and as soon as the woman removes her hand, the hair is stray again, rebellious. It is as though Caleb, her own son, has been caught in a chrysalis of time and has resurfaced here, years later, at the small café only to remind her that she has left him behind.

Joanne gathers up her plate and her cup and smiles at the woman.

Out on the little patio behind the café, Joanne lights a cigarette and stands there staring at the back of the adjacent building – the graffiti scarred brick and urine stinking dumpsters. She wonders where Caleb is now. He would be nearly ten-years old. She tries to call up the last time that she saw him as she dropped him off at kindergarten. She wonders, as she has many times, what he makes of the whole situation, and then she thinks of Travis. Travis who was always so good to her and so good to Caleb. She wonders if they are still living in the same house and if he has remarried. Although she would be understandably jealous, she wouldn't be able to blame him if he did. The boy needed a mother after all.

She wonders if Travis may have married one of his co-workers. One of the teachers or administrators. A woman with a soft face and an easy laugh. A woman who was permanent and reliable. But the time seems too short for Travis to have gotten over her leaving. Joanne takes a long, last drag of her cigarette and crushes it out against the side of the dented can the employees use as an ashtray. She would have thought by now that someone would have tracked her down. Travis or a police officer or a private detective. But she has been careful. She makes her way past the quaint two-story houses and brick buildings of Granville.

She is no longer Rita and hasn't been for a long time. She tried to officially change her name, but the Granville Village Hall, with its sandy hued stone and angled roof, said there was nothing they could do since her only ID was an expired Texas Drivers' License. Thankfully, the café she works at now has agreed to call her Joanne. The café and most of the places she has worked at. She couldn't even count the number of places she has lived or the different jobs she has had over the years. Somehow, she has fallen into the current and been simply carried along by the progression of days and weeks and months and years.

Travis sits at the edge of the pool, dangling his feet into the cool water and watching his son and his friends toss a tennis ball back and forth, hopping and splashing from one end of the pool to the other. It is here that he has spent countless evenings watching the softly rippling water, thinking about Rita. He has thought about the things that he might have done wrong and the things that he might have said. But the therapist says that there is probably nothing that he could have done, and it was within Rita's right to leave. The therapist tells him not to chalk it up to the miscarriage. He tells Travis that it is okay to have these feelings of guilt and shame and anger. The whole thing is mitigated but not eradicated.

He is thankful that Caleb seems to have adjusted. The boy can barely remember his mother, and knows her mostly from the stories that Travis and Noni and Papa have told him. He knows her face only from fading photographs. But the boy has his own therapist and he seems remarkably well-adjusted despite her loss.

"Children are sometimes far more resilient than their parents." The therapist tells him. "They take things in stride. They don't have the same established routines and expectations that adults do. Surely Caleb misses Rita, but he hasn't the memory of her. To him, she is more of an abstract construction than a reality."

It's not the way that he imagined raising Caleb. He did not envision doing so alone, and he has joined a group of men in similar circumstances: single fathers. Fathers abandoned, their wives lost to death, or incarceration, or infidelity. Travis is the only one in the group whose wife has simply run away. At first, he is seen as a pariah. The men understand and don't understand. The distant nature of his peers was probably unintentional, he reasoned. These other men couldn't make sense of why Travis was there. It took a month of meetings, there in the basement of the old church, before they began to recognize that his sense of loss was really no different from their own.

Joanne returns to her small apartment, the studio place that she is renting in the cheaper district of town, not tremendously far from the café. She likes the walk, even when it is raining, cherishing the change in season that she never experienced in Texas. Sure, there had been the storms and the hurricanes, but this was different. These were timid storms that didn't have the anger or ire of the storms that blew in off the gulf. These were simply storms that matched her mood on most days. She sits on the second-hand couch that serves as her bed and wonders how much of this way of life has become a way to try and serve a penance. How much of it has become shear asceticism? She opens the window and climbs out onto the fire escape and watches the rain roil against the leaves of the high elms that grow along the street, buffering the road noise. She lights a cigarette and huddles into her sweatshirt and watches the tip of the cigarette glow amber as the paper crackles.

Maybe in the morning she will call the house in San Antonio. It is all making sense to her now. She left on a whim and she'll return the same way. And she will deal with the prospect of whether or not she is accepted there when she returns. There is no way of knowing for certain, of course, what the reaction will be. But she has spent too much time running and trying to experience the world and now all she wants is that sense of home to return to her. She wants the comfort of staying in the same bed every night. She flicks her cigarette over the railing and watches as it spirals, caught on the wind, carried out into the middle of the street where it winks out in one of the broad puddles that has gathered along the curb.

Back inside, she runs the shower and looks at herself in the mirror. Her face is thinner now, her eyes slung with bags from lack of sleep. She hasn't slept well since she left, each night her dreams dogged by things that she should have done. Not a night has passed since she hasn't dreamed of them in some way. Hasn't conjured up the images that she spends her days blocking out and ignoring. Hasn't been able to put all of it aside. The picture that she took with her when she left is now crisscrossed with creases that are so deep and white that they are scars across the image. Even Caleb's face has been mostly obliterated by the constant abrasion in her pocket or in her backpack. She has shown the photo to no one. Not once over the four years that she has been gone has she told a single soul about her family or about where she is from or why she left.

As she runs the shower and stands beneath the steady stream of hot water, she looks at the stretch marks on her belly – an indelible reminder of a different time and a different self. But the marks will not wash away, and neither will the past. She wonders if she has the strength to return now, and convinces herself that she must, but she is uncertain as to whether the return will be for her or for Travis and Caleb. Perhaps they have long since dealt with her leaving and the return will only stir up old trauma, like pulling a scab from a wound. But she knows that the only thing that she can do is return. There is no avoiding it.

When she finally lies down on the couch, she feels the same fatigue and exhaustion settling into her body. A fatigue that she has felt for countless days. But there is a difference. There is a release as she curls into the couch and pulls the old blankets up over her body. For the first time in four years, she sleeps without nightmares. She sleeps straight through the night and, in the morning, it is the sun through the uncontained windows that wakes her and she is surprised to find that she has actually slept. The clock reads just after nine in the morning and she considers calling San Antonio. The phone number is tattooed on her mind. But she will not call.

Joanne calls the landlord and tells him that she will be leaving, and that she will leave the key and the rent on the table. The furniture is his to do with as he pleases. She thanks him for his kindness and calls down to the café and tells them that she appreciates the job, and that she has enjoyed working there over the past six months, but she has to leave. She has a family emergency she has to attend to. It's not entirely untrue.

Her feet guide her to the Greyhound station that she has walked past hundreds of times since arriving in the city. These bus stations are the hub of her existence, and the highways and freeways and back roads are the currier of her reality. Her currency has become miles and days. She stands patiently in line, lighter, easier, and happier than she remembers ever having been, and buys a ticket as directly to San Antonio as she can. It will take the better part of two days to get there but she doesn't care now. She has grown so accustomed to the busses and the routes that it feels like native territory, as if she were born of it and for it.

As she waits for her bus to depart, she stops by the small gift store in the terminal and buys a bag of trail mix and a bottle of water and a stuffed teddy bear that she will give to Caleb. She knows that he is too old for such things now and that the gesture will seem nothing if not paltry, but it will be something. It will be some small gesture that will be coupled with her return, and if in returning they want her to leave again, she will know that at least she is not completely unmoored from that reality. Rita will have been completely obliterated – stricken from the history of the earth, or maybe left only as a minor footnote. And Joanne will go off and find a place to settle. To be settled. To have a new and permanent life, which is all she really wants now. It's the only thing that she can look forward to in her world.

The bus pulls up and she gathers her bags and boards it, taking a seat, as usual, mid-way back on the driver's side of the bus. She no longer bothers looking at the other passengers. She is no longer curious who they are or where they are headed or if they have similar thoughts and feelings and fears. All she cares about is the return to a house that she hopes is still there, to a husband and a son who she has struggled to forget and now cannot help but remember in every possible, vivid detail she can conjure.

She wakes as the bus jumbles and shakes from the potholes and uneven road. Cities whisk past her window. She wonders how many times people have passed by San Antonio, or even their houses, and imagined the lives of complete strangers. She has been in the periphery of other peoples' worlds, just as they have been in the periphery of hers since she left. There is no antidote for anonymity, only a heartfelt embrace of that truth. It all seems so antithetical to her now as she stares out the window and the rain starts to come down, sparkling the glass with rough-hewn diamonds of water.

State borders slip by and she tries to imagine how many more miles and how many more minutes and hours before she returns home. It will be early morning when she arrives. Already it is late and the other passengers are falling asleep in the warm womb of the bus.

The bus jostles and she is awake again. The rain has picked up and the road is blackened to a slick sheen. She sits up and glances to where the driver sways in his seat. At first, she thinks that he is reaching for something beside him, and then she realizes from his sudden jerks and starts that he is nodding off. She has seen this before in drivers. They drive endless routes, although she's learned there is some sort of limit to the number of hours they can drive. A policy to ensure that the drivers don't fall asleep at the wheel. She will get up and walk to the front of the bus and talk to the driver to keep him awake. She swings her feet down from the seat and slips on her shoes, mesmerized for a moment by the way that the light shimmers off of the crenulated flooring. And then she is pulling herself up into the aisle and making her way forward as the bus shudders over the edge of the road where the little rumble strip is set to keep drivers awake. And as she glances up, still several rows back, the driver jerks awake again and in shock heaves the wheel over into oncoming traffic. The man's thin, silver hair, catches the light as the bus careens sideways.

At home in San Antonio, Travis is sitting down for breakfast with Caleb. It's a Saturday, and like so many other Saturdays they have a standing agreement to plan not to make plans and they will take the day as it comes. He knows that this is something that the boy will be missing ever since Rita disappeared one spring afternoon. The private detective that he hired followed her as far as Idaho and then lost the trail. Something had changed, and after several months of looking, Corbett insisted that there was little else that he could do.

"I'm good, but it turns out your wife has turned into a ghost. Somehow, she completely fell off of the map. I can't go on taking your money, I have to be honest, it's not in good faith."

Travis is exhausted. The constant optimism has worn on him. For two years he had held onto the hope that every time the phone rung it would be good news. He fantasized that Corbett would be on the other end of the line saying that he had found something. He needed something, anything, to justify the almost complete depletion of his son's college fund. He will keep spending until the money is gone. Caleb is only twelve. There will be plenty of time to rebuild the account, especially if he can locate Rita. After all, Noni and Papa will want to help with the boy's education, and, for his part, Caleb is a good student, a strong student even, so he should have all the prospects he needs.

The two of them are at the table, chatting idly over their bacon and eggs. Caleb has asked if he can have a cup of coffee and Travis has acquiesced. Not a big cup of coffee. A small cup, with milk and no sugar. The boy will have to build up to the thick, dark coffee that his father drinks. But it will happen. He knows that it is only a matter of time, the boy is already growing up so quickly, showing Rita's independent streak. But they have an understanding, the two of them, and they mediate their differences through their respective therapists, and the once a month, family therapists. In all honesty, more money has gone to therapy than to Corbett.

And so, he is surprised – still gnawing on a strip of fatty bacon – when the phone rings and he glances down and sees Corbett's number. It's been the better part of a year and a half since they spoke, and then it was only when Corbett said that he was eliminating the balance remaining on the account. He couldn't bring himself to charge Travis any more than he already had.

He wipes his hands on his jeans and answers the phone, instinctively walking into the hallway, so as to diffuse the conversation from his son. He's been practicing this for years. At first it was to hide the truth from his son, but as soon as it became inevitable, he told Caleb everything, and Caleb had, on several occasions, met Corbett when the detective came by the house. Now, it's only because he has to keep his optimism from his son.

"Howdy," he says into the phone, biting back the hope that there is something that has finally broken in the case. Perhaps Rita will finally be coming home.

"Travis, it's Corbett."

"I know. How are you?"

In a very Corbett fashion, he gets straight to the point, ignoring small talk. "Well, I don't know how to say this, but I'll tell you it's not good news."

Travis drifts into the living room. He can tell by the man's voice that whatever the news he has is laden with a weight too heavy for either of them to carry.

"What is it?"

"Rita's dead," Corbett says finally.

Travis shakes his head. Has he actually heard him, right? Perhaps Corbett, in his extension of conscientiousness, has decided that it would be best if he created the illusion that Rita is dead. Perhaps it is a metaphorical death.

"I know you can't find her, Corbett, we went over this."

There is a silence on the line.

"You didn't find her, did you?"

"In a manner of speaking. She is dead, though. I'm trying to tell you. There was a Greyhound bus headed out of Ohio, headed back towards

San Antonio. The state patrol says that the driver must have fallen asleep at the wheel. I'm sorry, Travis. Rita was thrown from her seat, or maybe she was already standing, when the bus cut across traffic and rolled. She was killed almost immediately."

Travis can feel the presence of Caleb in the hall and glances up to see his son. His beautiful son. He wishes that Caleb reminded him—at least physically, more of his wife. But he is a different person, a stranger in his own right as he begins to create his own identity. Travis feels the tears on his face, but is unaware that he is crying until he feels the drip run along his chin.

"Travis?"

"I'm here. How did you find out?"
Even after the contract ended, Corbett had kept his feelers out, passively listening because it was all too easy to pay attention to the grape vine. There were several other cases that he had done this for over the years. People who had disappeared or run away, and he'd found it beneficial over the years to pay attention. That morning, there had been a police report about the rollover and not long after that an old police friend had called to tell him that an ID had come up, something that they had flagged several years back.

"Joanne," Corbett says, "that was her middle name."

Travis nods before he realizes that he hasn't said anything and finally utters a small noise of affirmation.

"You can be certain that it's her though? Not some case of coincidence, some case of similar names."

"They found her Social Security Card as well. Matches her number. Sitting there in a bag that no one else claimed. The police realized quickly that it must have been hers."

"So it's official?"

There's another long, awkward silence on the other end of the line.

"Corbett?"

"That's the other thing that I was calling about, Travis. They need someone to come down and ID the remains. Look, I'm coming by, I'm already headed your way. I'll drive you up there. You and the boy."

Travis is already staggering to his feet, wondering what he will tell his son. Can he avoid it? Can he avoid telling his only son that the mother he barely remembers was killed while, at least theoretically, on her way back home to see them. On top of that, can he tell his son that the detective is coming by their house to drive them north for hours in order to identify the body of a woman that he has never really known? Dropping the phone on the table, he turns now towards where Caleb has been watching him from the hallway.

Shattered Pieces of Sun

It isn't until Noni pulls into the driveway in Corpus Christi that she realizes it is the longest day of the year. When Rita was a little girl, the two of them spent the Summer Solstice standing on the shore with the breeze buffeting against them, white-capping the distant water. Eventually the sun would begin its final decent towards the horizon where it seemed to melt into the ocean. There'd been another summer, years later, after Caleb was born, that they had returned to the beach as a family. There in the driveway, as she cuts the engine, it's this memory that returns, nostalgia sharpened, to her mind.

The plastic wheels of her suitcase grumble over the driveway, and once inside the house a cool stillness settles around her. Stan has gone to the tavern for the evening, that she knows for sure, but she no longer cares. Rita's disappearance has driven a wedge between them – an invisible thing like the same poles of a magnet creating an unbridge-able field.

"Ask me, that girl ran away because of Travis. No woman up and leaves her family for any other reason."

But this was to be expected. Rita was, after all, only his step-daughter. He would have

reacted differently had it been Stacy that
disappeared. But the arguments are months old
now and the increase in blood pressure isn't
worth the breath spent on it. Perhaps Stan even
relishes these long weekends without her
around – bachelor weekends. He hasn't bothered
to comment on her long trips up to Austin to
help Travis with Caleb.

She is exhausted from the long ride. She
slips out of her clothes and showers, letting the
cool water run over her skin and scalp, dressing
again in jeans and a faded flannel shirt.
Standing in the kitchen, she glances at the clock
above the stove; in nearly two hours the longest
day of the year will end.

The beach is only fifteen minutes away, and
she knows that there will be stragglers there.
Elsewhere in the city, people are either unaware
that it is the longest day or they don't care.
Perhaps there will be vacationing families that
have come down for their early summer retreat.
Canoodling lovers and young couples with kids
in tow, lounging on blankets and towels, or
perched in camp chairs. Dogs running rampant
on the sand, kicking up little sprays of dust and
shaking saltwater from their fur.

Despite herself, she is looking forward to
this – as though some simple part of it will bring
her closer to her missing daughter. She refuses
to let herself think that maybe Rita will be there

on the beach, sitting on a blanket near their old spot, staring to the west where the water meets the sky. It will be enough for her to see that life continues for other people, and the pain that she feels is masked by her own soft smile. Well practiced Southern manners has bred into her the ability to hide her own shame and pain. It is bit back and buried deep beneath gentility.

The water carries shattered pieces of sun in ripples towards the shore as she finds a park bench and watches strangers oblivious to her own pain. Not far away, there are lovers strolling who may only be together for a week or a month or a year. An older couple twine hands faithfully, at least until one of them passes away, plunging the other into a bottomless depression. A dog, now spry, runs around until he will eventually become incontinent on the living room floor and have to be put down.

"Lord Jesus," she whispers without knowing how to continue.

This is how tragedy affects people, she thinks; it drags beauty and hope and love from even the most casual observations. But if today is the longest day of the year – the day that will contain the largest amount of suffering – then she knows that it must be balanced by the shortest day of the year. She breathes in the crisp salt air, feels the wind tug at her jacket. Feels the goosebumps crawl up her shoulders.

Feels as though she has always known that people hide such pain. In years past, she would bend a careful ear towards those who seem to be in pain, offering what comfort she could. But she refused to be a burden. Here on the beach, she harbors the sadness in her heart and lets the cool wind cool her, ground her. She lets the ocean air breathe her in for a change. The sun casts brilliant oranges and pinks against the sky as it begins to burn a hole in the ocean along the horizon. Noni lingers there as the sky turns dark blue and eventually black. The breeze has calmed down by the time she walks back to her car.

In her absence, the house has retained its cool stillness, and, for a moment, she wonders what it would be like if Stan had disappeared. What would she do if she were to return home and find him missing? Would she spend the evening calling friends and relatives and local hospitals? Perhaps she would think that he had lost his mind, and she would drive the streets looking for her husband. She would find him wandering in his bathrobe and skivvies near the park; disorientation would be imprinted on his face and he would look at her like a stranger. Wary. Afraid.

A small part of her relishes the fantasy that he would be gone. That she would have something that would be an apparent reason for sympathy. The neighbors would talk about her missing husband – missing either physically or mentally. She would become one of those beautiful sainted women who suffer through things like this with decorum and grace. But, in the end, she knows that he is at the tavern playing poker and that he will return home smelling of rye and cigars. He will shower, standing beneath the hot stream of water until his skin is lobster pink, and he will crawl into bed and be fast asleep and snoring almost before she has the time to say goodnight.

Lately, she has begun to understand why her daughter might have disappeared. Before, she had tried hundreds of times to find a reason. She has thought about the catalyst – the trigger and motivation of such a disappearance, turning over in her mind all of the reasons that a person might choose to walk away from a perfect life. A nice house. A loving husband. A sweet child. She had examined every possible motive for fissures. Finding none, she grew only more frustrated. Now, she imagines packing a single backpack and walking back out to her car. It would be the better part of two days before Stan would discover that she was not at their son-in-law's house, and then would he call the hospitals and friends and relatives? But it is only a daydream. She can't imagine really leaving because she can't imagine where she would go. It's one of the primary things that she can't seem to wrap her mind around. There is no way of knowing where it was that Rita was heading to or thought she was heading to. The only thing that she can imagine is that Rita just needed to leave. She needed to escape from her situation for one reason or another. Tedium or sadness. The sadness of tedium.

Noni retrieves the bottle of rye from the liquor cabinet and pours herself a stiff drink. Perhaps tonight she will be the one that is asleep and snoring before Stan comes home. Stepping out onto the porch, she inhales the smell of mesquite and cut grass. She is still in her oversized flannel and as she sits on the porch swing and tightens the kerchief over her hair, at first unaware of the headlights washing over the porch. It's far too soon for Stan to be home, and when she looks at the car that has pulled into the drive she realizes it's not Stan at all, it's Stacy's Ford Ranger, it's dented front-fender reflecting the porchlight like a cataract. She has completely forgotten that her step-daughter was coming home for the summer — completely forgot that finals were done this week.

"Hey mama," Stacy says, dropping her purse on the porch and smoothly slipping the glass away from Noni's hand. She sips and leans back

in the swing, the chain creaking lightly against
the eyebolts.

"What a drive," she says.

"You go pour yourself one, dear," Noni says.

Stacy sits for a moment and takes another
long pull off of Noni's drink before handing it
back, the ice tinkling lightly against the glass.

"Might as well bring the bottle."

The screen door bangs shut behind her and
the girl is inside. Noni stands and stretches. Her
back has tightened, probably from the several
hours that she spent on the beach, and she can
feel the dryness of her skin where it has pulled
taught against her cheek bones. She stares out
over the yard. Inhales the mesquite again and
stares at the tire swing hanging from the old
elm at the front of the yard. Stacy knows that
Rita has been gone for months now. They were
step-siblings, but once they'd been as close as
any two real sisters could hope to be. The age
gap between them safely situated Rita in a
peaceful place as a sister nearly ten years older.

How long had the two girls spent lingering
in the front yard – Stacy swinging in lazy circles
while Rita painted her toenails on an unfurled
blanket, the two girls chattering and giggling.
Their legs sun- darkened from hours in the sun
and lazing on the porch until Stan had yelled at
them to go about their chores. And now, one

daughter has disappeared into the ether and the other returns home. She admonishes herself silently for wishing it was the other daughter that had emerged suddenly in the driveway. No. She will appreciate the time that she has with Stacy.

It is the two of them out on the porch sipping from sweating glasses of bourbon, the bottle on the porch beneath the swing. Noni can feel her cheeks flush with alcohol. She can't remember the last time that she was drunk — for a year that has been solely Stan's domain, although he would never call it drunk. He always seems to call it maintaining or stabilizing. She thinks of the time that her own husband disappeared from her life, and although she hasn't said anything to Travis, she knows something of the feeling even if it is far from identical. She vacillates between calling it sympathy and empathy. George had not left suddenly, nor had his leaving been spontaneous or one-sided. It had been a joint thing. An agreement that they would forever be disagreeing if there was no end to the relationship that had begun when the two of them were both still in high school. He'd been an accountant. Not at first of course, but he had worked for one of the big oil companies in the area and had made good money. Money that allowed them to buy the house that she still lives in. He had left her with the house and a daughter and taken an apartment in Raleigh, where he had moved to pursue his new job and a girlfriend that was ten years younger.

"Oh, how we argued," Noni is telling Stacy now, although she isn't certain how she got on the topic in the first place.

"Everyone argues, mama."

"Well, some do, some don't. We argued like cats and dogs most every night of the week. It was one of those things we rushed into. Think back to when you had been dating Danny."

Stacy groans and smiles and sips her whiskey.

"Think about any number of boys that you dated in high school, even though we or Rita had warned you against it. Did that stop you? Did it change your mind? No. And y'all enjoyed each other's company at the time. Liked spending time with each other."

"Nothing wrong with that."

"Nothing at all. I'm not saying that there is. But young lust is not the same as young love. Young lust is like gasoline on a fire. Burns hot and bright."

"So they say."

"Do they? I thought I'd come up with that all on my own."

Noni gets to her feet unsteadily, having to lift herself from the swing to keep her head from swaying. The heat of the day and the lack of food and the long drive have gotten to her. She is beyond caring what Stan will say when he gets home from Poker. She is dimly aware of Stan entering the room. The digital numbers on the clock are a dim green blur, and she squints one eye shut to make out the numbers. It is well after midnight and her head feels like lead.

"Christ Jesus," Stan says and she can hear his car keys and loose change splash against the nightstand, "you say I smell like a distillery."

"Love you, too."

The bed moves beneath his weight, tipping downwards, creating a gravity that pulls her towards the center of the bed. The warmth of the blankets is displaced by the cool air of Stan slipping beneath the covers.

"Since when do you get drunk?"
"Only maintaining," she says.

"Since when do you maintain?"
"You're aware that my daughter is missing."

There is silence. She knows that the mention of Rita has sucked the air out of the conversation, creating a hermetic seal. She is awake now, however, and she heaves herself out of bed and down to the kitchen where she pours herself a glass of water from the tap and sits at the table in the darkness, staring at the large elm tree in the front yard. The tire swing hangs straight down, a monument for a missing daughter.

Acknowledgments

Those that most deserve thanks are often those most likely to be embarrassed by their identification. But, damnit, I'm going to do it anyways. I thank: my wife and for her enduring support. I thank my daughter, for her inevitable curiosity and tenacity. I think my parents, grandparents, and relatives too numerous (or infamous) to name.

And, of course, my colleagues and fellow writers, without whom I would feel I had no community. I am, of course, indebted to my mentors at Hollins University: Richard Dillard, Cathy Hankla, David Huddle, and Liz Poliner. To those at Unsolicited Press, this book would quite literally not exist without you.

And lastly, an of those who unlikely to ever read this: thank you to Don Delillo, Michael Ondaatje, Charles D'Ambrosio, Hunter Thompson, and Ernest Hemingway.

About the Author

Michael Overa was born and raised in the Pacific Northwest. After completing his MFA at Hollins University Michael returned to Seattle where he currently works as a writing tutor and is a writer-in-residence with Seattle's Writers in The Schools Program. His work has appeared in the *Portland Review, East Bay Review, Fiction Daily, Inlandia,* and *Across the Margin,* among others.

An Interview with Michael Overa

What literary journeys have you gone on?

Lately I've gotten back into audio books. I do quite a bit of driving, and it's nice to have something other than the radio to listen to. Librivox does a pretty fantastic job at providing public domain content. The journey really ends up being one of listening to books I haven't read in ages (or perhaps never read).

What is the first book that made you cry?

Not to sound overtly masculine, but I don't remember a book ever making me cry. I have been deeply affected by books before – two that stand out to me are Tim O'Brien's <u>The Things They Carried</u> and <u>Blood Meridian</u> by Cormac McCarthy. More recently I had a rather visceral response to several of the scenes in Margaret Atwood's <u>The Handmaid's Tale.</u>

Does writing energize or exhaust you?

I'd say it's a little bit of both. Some days it feels like you're on fire and coming off of a writing session is an absolute high. Other days it feels like a slog. Regardless, even a marathon session can eventually be exhausting. Those days that are a slog sometimes end up productive, simply because I feel like I'm grumpier with my own work.

What are common traps for aspiring writers?

Having worked with a lot of young writers over the years, I've noticed that a lot of folks feel compelled to get everything right on the first attempt. The big myth is that writing (and many other forms of art) is that everything falls into place in a divine fit of inspiration. It's a myth, I think, based on the illusion that artists create. Our audience only sees the final polished product, not the endless drafts and struggles and cursing that preceded that final product. However, I also feel that it is a dangerous myth for practitioners, because it can lead to paralysis of the pen.

Does a big ego help or hurt writers?

I think a big ego can hurt anyone – especially artists. My conviction is that when an artist's ego gets too big they are no longer concerned with quality and craft as they once were. There's an illusion of the Midas Touch that comes with too big an ego. I think to be successful, to move forward and be a good artist, you have to keep a healthy awareness of potential failure. The easiest thing for a reader to do is to stop reading, and, I think, if you don't preserve a healthy dose of that fear, you run the risk of lowering your standards.

Have you ever gotten reader's block?

I don't think so. There seem to be occasions when I'm walking through a bookstore that I'm momentarily overwhelmed by the number of things that I could read – but that's more akin to going to a restaurant and trying to decide what to order.

Did you ever consider writing under a pseudonym?

I have, but only recently. I'm tinkering with a sort of YA dystopian story, and it seems to me that it would be better served (and better serve my other writing) if it were not connected directly to my primary work. This is not to say that I disparage such things.

Do you think someone could be a writer if they don't feel emotions strongly?

I think anyone can be a writer. I don't think that emotion is necessarily key, so much as introspection and precision of thought. I suppose it's a question of empathy. It seems that good writers are empathic people. I suppose it's also a question of being a "sensitive soul." One could argue that people like Hemingway and Woolf were successful primarily out of an awareness of their own vulnerability.

What other authors are you friends with, and how do they help you become a better writer?

I always wish that I had more writer friends. I have the great fortune, however, to work with a good number of writers through Seattle's Writers In The Schools program. All of my writer friends humble me, rather incidentally, by being such fantastic writers. It's easy to question your own skill when those around you are so profoundly talented. I don't know if this is common for most writers, but I'm rather introverted, and have a hard time maintaining relationships, simply because I go off into my own little world.

Do you want each book to stand on its own, or are you trying to build a body of work with connections between each book?

I would like each book to stand on its own; it seems to me that there will be an inevitable arc or connection between different works. I think of Hemingway or Atwood or McCarthy, all seem to have a clear progression of ideas. I guess I would also worry that, were I to focus on the entire opus, I would lose sight of the individual work. It seems to me that, in order to follow an authentic artistic development, one can't try to plan too far ahead of the current project.

What was the best money you ever spent as a writer?

Over the years I've spent a lot of money on developing craft. I've travelled to writing conferences, bought books on craft, attended lectures, and completed my MFA. Often I'm somewhat jealous of artists and musicians who have all sorts of physical tools at their disposal. However, I think writers are lucky to have simple artistic needs. We need only our minds. However, for my money the best investment has been pocket notebooks. I like being able to grab a little book out of my pocket and scribble down an idea or a line or a word. They become these little treasure troves for later. I've used a variety of these over the years, but, lately, I'm quite fond of Field Notes because they're slim and relatively inexpensive.

What authors did you dislike at first but grew into?

Umberto Eco for sure. I tried to get through In The
Name of the Rose when I was at college. It wasn't
until a good seven or eight years later (at graduate
school) that I read <u>The Mysterious Flame of Queen
Loana</u> and was struck by his cleverness. Which is
not to say that Eco is merely a clever writer. I think
he's a writer's writer. I think that he has
tremendous range and technical ability. The fact
that he has a great imagination doesn't hurt either.
**What was an early experience where you
learned that language had power?**

I have vivid memories of my mother telling my
brother and I that we weren't allowed to use words
unless we knew what they meant. This lead to a
fascination with words and, on some occasions,
scouring he dictionary for words I could use to insult
my brother surreptitiously.

What's your favorite under-appreciated novel?

One of my favorite books of all time is Don Delillo's
<u>The Body Artist</u>. It's a short novel, and not one that
many people have heard of. The opening sequence is
subtle and slow, but so fantastically authentic. I
reread the book about once a year, and have done so
(more or less) for the past fifteen years or so.

**How do you balance making demands on the
reader with taking care of the reader?**

I don't think too much about the reader. Andrew
Stanton has a great TED talk in which he discusses
what he calls the Unifying Theory of 2+2. The idea
is to make the reader work for "their meal" without

letting them know that they're working for it. The
closest I come to really thinking of the reader is
when I try to balance being too subtle against being
too obvious.

**As a writer, what would you choose as your
mascot/avatar/spirit animal?**

I'd have to say my spirit animal/mascot would have
to be Boxer, the horse from Orwell's Animal Farm.
I've always identified with Boxer – his slavish
commitment to the greater good. I feel that I've often
approached writing the same way that Boxer
approaches his role on the farm: I simply have to
work harder.

**What do you owe the real people upon whom
you base your characters?**

It's rare that I could clearly identify a single
character that is based upon a real person. Often the
characters are such composites that I'm not exactly
sure who the character is based on. That said, there
is a character in a my upcoming collection This
Endless Road who is modeled on my grandfather.
It's loose, but I definitely used him as a template.
Sadly he passed away a while back. The character is,
essentially, an homage.

**How many unpublished and half-finished
books do you have?**

Hard to say. At present there must be at least three.
One, my first novel, is really close to being finished.
I'm hoping that after This Endless Road I can shift
my attention to the novel.

What does literary success look like to you?

Any time a stranger says: "I really liked your story" I
feel that I have succeeded. I mean, when it isn't in
the awkwardness of passing. I mean when a
complete stranger comes up to me after a reading
just to tell me that they liked it. When someone goes
out of their way to give you a compliment it rings
more true than anything else. I imagine I might be
equally honored if someone took the time to come up
to me and tell me how much they detested a
particular piece of work.

What's the best way to market your books?

I've tried most things – but I don't know what works
best. The one that I enjoy the most is giving copies of
books to friends and acquaintances who I know read
and read well. My colleagues, I feel, are the ones
most likely to recommend my work to someone else,
especially if they enjoy it.

What kind of research do you do, and how long
do you spend researching before beginning a
book?

I research simultaneously. Often, in fact, I think I
don't really start researching until I have a couple
thousand words down. I feel like I have to get the lay
of the land before I find out what I need to know –
otherwise I try and put in everything that I've
learned, and it's harder to be selective.

How many hours a day do you write?

Ideally I would write an hour a day. At present I work three jobs and have a toddler. I've been working mostly on editing my current work and pondering other work. In the meantime I read. Hopefully I'll be able to remedy this soon. Two jobs seems like a cakewalk.

What period of your life do you find you write about most often?

I think the period of say twenty to thirty is the age range of most of my characters. I don't know if there's a specific reason for that. I somewhat assume that the age I write about will shift as I get older.

How do you select the names of your characters?

I don't have any specific sort of process. If a name doesn't come to me at first I use a generic name as a place holder. Often as the story evolves a better name seems to fit. Otherwise female characters end up Sara or Anna, and male characters end up John or Alex. Why those specific names? No idea.

If you didn't write, what would you do for work? And if writing isn't your "day job", what are you currently doing to pay the bills?

Writing is, at present, connected to the work I do to pay the bills. I teach English at a local community college here in Seattle, and also work as a private tutor. Until recently I was also a writer in residence for Seattle's Writers In The Schools (WITS program). I made the tough decision to take a break from WITS in order to spend more time with my family

and more time writing. For a period of about five
years I worked as a bartender, and I would say that
bartending was incredibly conducive to a writing
life. Most people think it was conducive because of
the interaction with patrons. Actually, it was simply
the fact that I only worked four days a week and
never had to take work home with me.

**What one thing would you give up to become a
better writer?**

I'd probably give a up a good number of things if
there was a guarantee that it would help me develop
my craft. I wouldn't give something up in a Deal
With the Devil sort of way, because I'd want to
actually know that I'd exchanged a vice of some sort
for an improvement. I suppose pizza and beer would
be sacrifices that I would surrender.

What is your favorite childhood book?

My dad signed us up for some sort of Disney Classics
program when I was a kid. It seemed like we got a
book in the mail every month or so. I loved getting
those books in the mail (this was, by the way, way
before the Internet). I don't think the two books that
stand out were part of this, but I also vividly
remember reading to myself Black Beauty and the a
children's version of the myths of Hercules.

**Does your family support your career as a
writer?**

I've been fantastically lucky to have a family that
supports my work. Both my parents encouraged my
early writing and reading pursuits. I remember

showing them stories I'd written in first or second grade. Thankfully there was never any pressure from them to pursue a specific path or career. My wife is likewise supportive – I can't imagine a better partner. Our daughter, however, would rather I lie on the floor and play than write; perhaps one day she'll become more supportive.